Michael Pollick's Proving Ground

Michael Pollick

Published by Michael Pollick, 2024.

MICHAEL POLLICK'S PROVING GROUND

First edition. April 24, 2024.

Copyright © 2024 Michael Pollick.

ISBN: 979-8224652778

Written by Michael Pollick.

Michael Pollick's Proving Ground

copyright 2024 by Michael Pollick
All Rights Reserved

WOODLAND ELEMENTARY SCHOOL: PLAYGROUND CONFIDENTIAL

Woodland Elementary School came with its own proving ground, although outsiders often wrote it off as nothing more than a simple PLAYground. Those of us who ran through that unforgiving and cruel jungle know better. The playground at Woodland was actually a bit schizophrenic. There were sections designated as safe for grades K-3, then other areas deemed suitable. for the more discerning 4th to 6th grade crowd. This 38th parallel was never actually marked with a physical line on the asphalt or anything, but the younger kids instinctively knew when they were getting perilously close to crossing over it. It was Stow's version of a prison shock collar, only without the explosive charges. The K-3 crowd had to content themselves with games like hopscotch, which was barely a game in the first place, and the dreaded *small* swings. The teeter-totters were also divided between amateur and professional grade, although the one "game" that became universal was the sudden jump from the lower position, allowing gravity to take care of the victim in the higher position.

One popular playground game evolved from the innocent version we all played in the school's so-called multipurpose room. For a while, it was the gym for indoor PE classes, then it morphed into the lunchroom for meals, then became a gym again until the artistic urge took over and it became the auditorium for school talent shows or outside performances or whatever. While it was still a gym, however, we played the game known as dodge ball. Dodge ball was the straightforward version—there's a ball, dodge it. There was a natural upper limit to how much pepper could be put on those odd rubber balls only sold to schools, apparently. Throw, dodge, retrieve, throw again, hit, leave. These were all graspable concepts to a 4th grader.

Somewhere along the way, dodge ball became fire ball. Fire ball was similar to dodge ball only in the sense that fast pitch baseball was similar to slow pitch softball. Fire ball was serious business, played by serious people. I remember one guy at Kimpton Middle School who could pick off any target of his choosing from across the entire gym floor. You could try to catch the ball, you could try to get out of the way, you could try to feign injury and leave, but Mark was eventually going to nail you with that fire ball. Death by round rubber was in the cards. Once Mark got through picking off most of the opposing team, one unfortunate survivor who spent the entire game hiding behind others would be the last one standing. The PE teacher would declare a free fire zone, meaning there were no more lines standing between competitors. Mark would stalk his prey for a few minutes, then deliver a crushing blow from three feet away. I think we ended up giving Mark both ears and the tail one time.

There was another game which was actually banned by the principal during my time at Woodland. Many of us can still remember the last words we heard before our collective lights went out: "Red Rover, Red Rover, let Mikey come over!". Red Rover was definitely a team sport, with two lines of players facing each other from a distance. The idea was to link arms and form an impenetrable human chain. A captain would select a challenger from the other side and lead his or her team in the taunting chant "Red Rover, Red Rover, let (insert name here) come over!". With that simple request, Inserted Name would try to break through the chain by any means necessary. If he or she was successful, a player would be sent back to the other side. If he or she could not break through, they became the newest link in that chain.

This process of brute force elimination could stretch on for a while, I remember.

The Red Rover rot set in after more than a few Insert Names Here came on over as requested and failed miserably. Either they got clotheslined by the strongest links, or they inadvertently took out a few links of their own during an open field tackle situation. The Red Rover victim-to-champion ratio became far too lopsided for the principal's liking, so he sent out a general bulletin that our Red Rover playing days were over. I remember a few people were sorely disappointed that their best head-butting days were now behind them, but it was a banner day for Insert Names Here everywhere.

One afternoon at Woodland, I watched two of our janitors drill a hole in the playground blacktop. They installed a tall aluminum pole and anchored it into the ground with cement. One of the janitors attached a long string to a hook at the very top of the pole, then attached what appeared to be a volleyball to the other end of the string. Without much fanfare, the internationally ignored sport of tetherball had come to Stow. None of us knew exactly how the game was supposed to be played, but eventually the PE teacher did take us outside and explained the basic rules of tetherball. At long last, here was a game that made as little sense as possible and we actually stood in line waiting to play it. The best part was that helpless feeling at the very end as you watched your opponent wrap that ball around the pole at lightning speed.

One version of tetherball started out as a straight punch service, with the goal being to get past the other player and wrap the entire cord around the pole in a certain direction. This could be done through brute force or finesse, depending on the player's anger management skills. The other version called for the ball to swing slowly around the pole a few times in one player's direction, and then players could pounce on the ball at will. This was the version of tetherball that confused me the most. What other game on Earth started with one team watching helplessly as the other team loaded most of the bases? That three-turn advantage was devilishly hard to overcome, yet we would dutifully watch the ball wind around the pole like lemmings until that third spin. Tetherball was clearly a game sold to school administrators, not to the kids.

One "game" unique to Woodland was not really a game at all, but more of a dare. The back of the school's designated playground extended into a small woods. In order to keep students from wandering too far into those woods, rings were painted on several trees to serve as borders. The woods on one side of those border trees looked pretty much like the woods on the other side, but rules were rules. We were NOT to travel beyond those ringed trees, ever ever ever. Of course, there was no faster way to get some of us to disobey a school rule than by telling us not to do it.

By the time I was in 5th grade, the mythology of the Land Beyond The Painted Trees had become huge. There were stories of evil men who kidnapped trespassing children, who were of course never seen again. That was a good one for me—I would sometimes even stand guard near the ringed trees and look for anyone even a little suspicious. There were also tales of bears or coyote packs hiding in those woods, just waiting for free kids meals. Perhaps the best deterrents were all of those apocryphal stories about the punishment that awaited anyone who was caught behind those trees. In the unspoken Woodland criminal codes, crossing over into the Forbidden Zone during school hours was at the top of the list. I knew a few people who paid dearly for that brief taste of life outside the compound. I found out later, however, that there was a nice little trail that ran through those woods, and it ended at one of the least scariest places in Stow—the Stow-Kent Shopping Center. The school system spent years scaring us away from Kresge's department store and the A&P.

HAVE THE SIRENS STOPPED SCREAMING, CLARICE?
The Stow 4th of July Parade, Sponsored by Beltone.

The Victorians essentially perfected the Christmas holiday season, and the Puritans put a clear thumbprint on the celebration we now call Thanksgiving. However, the city of Stow OWNED the 4th of July; the competition was and still is for second place. Other cities may think they can assemble an acceptable bevy of Shriner midget cars, high school bands, beauty queens and themed floats, but when I was a child in the early 1970s, the Stow, Ohio Fourth of July parade operated on a completely different plane of existence. Route 59 through town became the epicenter of a 3 hour tribute to the civic duty gods.

The parade started assembling at the Stow-Kent Shopping Center, which was really the only location on that end of the street capable of supporting so many parade entrants. The parade route was one street running east to west, terminating at a review stand several miles away in the so-called downtown section of Stow. The mayor and other dignitaries would congregate at that review stand, but most of us regular folk would find a spot along Kent Road, pull out an old-school lawn chair and wait for clear signs of an impending parade. We usually didn't have to wait long. A few police officers on motorcycles would clear the stragglers off the street just before the largest peace time armada of emergency vehicles ever assembled started the festivities.

In the annals of historically bad ideas, one immediately springs to mind: Assembling a collection of fire trucks and ambulances from a three county area and having them drive single-file down the same stretch of densely populated highway. The CONCEPT of seeing a fleet of shiny fire trucks driving down our street sounded promising indeed to a 6 year old. However, the execution was a completely different story. As part of the parade ritual, all of these emergency vehicles decided to turn on their lights and sirens at the same time and for the same duration, which is to say, forever. The cumulative effect of all of those outside voices was a mind-numbing deafness, which lingered for the rest of the now-silent parade. To add audio insult to sonic injury, some of those fire engines also blew their diesel horns, which entered our bodies at the ear canal and exited out of places we forgot we had.

After the Beltone-sponsored parade of emergency vehicles passed by, life along the sidelines got a little easier. The American Field Service volunteers would walk up and down the parade route, hawking very small American flags that we would dutifully wave at the parade participants. For us kids, this was all leading up to the most important part of the parade: the candy toss. This was no small thing. Someone on a passing float would toss a handful of candy in our direction and a sugar-fueled feeding frenzy would begin. Every once in a while, an errant pitch would send the bulk of the candy in one direction and one direction only. Mine. Before I could pack up all of that Bubble Yum or Tootsie Roll booty, however, my mom would remind me of my Gallant tendencies and I'd end up redistributing it to the less fortunate. Darn the less fortunate.

One group that both scared and excited me was the Shriners, or as I thought of them, the old guys with the funny hats. At one point, their stunt vehicles of choice were Honda mini-bikes, which they would ride in intricate formations at different points along the route. Before going into their routine, however, a few of the flying monkey men would zip across the sidelines to make sure no groundlings were in the path of the mini-bikes. That little safety maneuver scared me to death, since I was often too busy picking up stray candy to notice a Shriner barreling down on top of me with 50 ccs of raw power behind him. The Shriners later switched to those miniature clown cars, which seemed to ratchet back the drama of non-athletic competition, in my younger opinion. You could only do so much damage in a clown car, and if these men thought riding mini-bikes designed for 8 year olds made them look like dorks on parade, the cars were not exactly babe wagons, either.

What happened next could only be described as an object lesson in terminal whiteness. The area high school bands would all march down the parade route in a stupefyingly predictable order: Majorettes, banner, drum major, band, band directors. Majorettes, banner, drum major, band, band directors. The upper funk limit for most of these bands was Stevie Wonder's "Sir Duke". Bands from Tallmadge, Hudson, Cuyahoga Falls, Kent and most notably, Stow, would take turns performing these squeaky tight Marvin the Martian arrangements of traditional march music and fight songs. Stow's fight song was the same as Ohio State's: "Across the Field" (alternative lyrics not included). Precision was the underlying theme, and for the most part we appreciated the homage to discipline and order. We were still Midwesterners, after all.

But nothing, NOTHING, prepared us for the volunteer drum corps from Akron. They wore purple and black uniforms, and clearly brought the funk from the county seat. No clarinets, no flutes, no saxophones; just trumpets and a boatload of drums. These guys didn't march in hyper-straight formations; they didn't really "march" at all. They eased on down the road with a solid BOOM-CHAKA-LAKA, BOOM-CHAKA-LAKA back beat driving them the whole way. As a young, frightened Caucasian, I had read the forbidden texts concerning funk, but during the Stow 4th of July parade, I actually had a chance to experience it in person. I liked it. I *really* liked it.

One of the more interesting, and one would think least innocent bystander-friendly, participants in the parade were the stunt shooters from Akron. At regular intervals along the route, a volunteer sitting in the back of an open-bed truck would hold out a balloon and shout "Fire!". At this point, the three trick shooters walking behind the truck would whip out their six-shooters and shoot the balloon dead. These people were lightning fast and extremely accurate, two qualities I admired in stunt shooters with live ammunition walking down a crowded street. I found out later that they only shot wax bullets, which would disintegrate on contact with the balloon. The version inside my eight-year-old mind was much better.

The floats were almost always from the "Red, White and Blaine" school of civic pride, and it was always interesting to see someone I knew from school or church strapped to one, but I noticed that some of my friends couldn't handle the pressures of sudden float fame. They would Bogart the candy, for one thing. After all we had been through from Kindergarten to July 3rd of that year, the least a buddy on a Stow Lions Club float could do was hook a brother up with that sweet, sweet Tootsie Roll action. Ingrates.

Perhaps nothing explains the Stowbilly psyche better than the ignoble end of all 4th of July parades. The parade participants who routinely gathered the most applause and adulation from the crowd weren't the high school bands, the gleaming and historical emergency vehicles or the local civic leaders. We saved our loudest cheers for the rows of street cleaners with their cheerfully waving drivers, who closed out the parade in style. Well, except for those of us who watched our last shot at Bazooka Joe and Dum Dums get swept away forever.

KIMPTON MIDDLE SCHOOL: Shh, I'm in the IRC becoming self-actualized.

From kindergarten until 6th grade, most of us Stowites attended the same elementary schools. We knew those places like the backs of our hands, and life during school time was mostly a matter of jumping through the hoops until the buses arrived. However, 7th grade was a completely different matter, and one that introduced apprehension to the curriculum. All of us who had previously identified as Woodlanders or Fishcreekers or Indian Trailers or whatever were now headed towards the One Middle School To Rule Over All, otherwise known as Kimpton. Preparing to go to Kimpton Middle School was the first inkling that recess as we knew it was indeed over.

Like a lot of other middle schools of its time, Kimpton subdivided its 7th and 8th grade students into instructional "teams". For students, this meant that we would be taught most of our subjects by the same four or five teachers assigned to our team. The team streams would rarely be crossed. I may have spent seven long years at Woodland with a guy on team 7-1, but from this point on I was a member of team 7-2, and who knows what sort of shocking Pagan rituals those 7-1 types performed on warm weekend nights? I had my own suspicions on how these teams were selected, but nothing I could actually prove at the time.

Kimpton was much larger than the narrow halls of Woodland, and its immenseness was not lost on a small potato like me. We would all congregate in the cafeteria area just before classes began, and the first few weeks were usually spent looking for anyone anywhere who used to attend the same elementary school we did. But that summer between 6th and 7th grade seemed to have an effect on many of us. Yes, I did go to that much smaller elementary school in an entirely different city with that guy over there, but that's where the similarities now ended. We were all Kimptonites now, a young adolescent example of *e pluribus, unum.* It was now all about the *team.* What *team* are you on? Who's on OUR team? I hope *that* kid isn't on MY team. Kimpton was the opening two years of the 2-2-2 educational top or bottom, bottom or top schizophrenia that defined Stow's philosophy on higher learning for decades.

Speaking of educational philosophy, one of my teachers at Kimpton explained the underlying concept behind the apparent madness of the team teaching system. Kimpton was built at a time when a behavioral psychologist named Maslow was the man of the hour. Maslow, unlike his draconian predecessor Benjamin Skinner, believed that students (like all of God's children) learned best when their basic human needs were met. Maslow developed a triangular chart that listed the "Hierarchy of Needs", from the concrete items such as food, water and shelter to those more esoteric needs such as peace, love and understanding. Maslow was obviously a pinko and a hippie, but I digress. Once a person had all of these needs met, which could take an hour or a lifetime, then he or she would enter a Nirvana-like state called "self-actualization". A self-actualized middle school student was a happy middle school student, and much less likely to become a burden on local taxpayers years later.

In order to follow the path, excuse me, Path of self-actualization, a student at Kimpton should have felt free to explore his or her outside environment without getting so hung up on society's rules, man. In reality, we still needed hall passes to meet a few basic human needs Maslow conveniently left off the chart. We didn't go to the Establishment's "library", with its buzz-killing due dates and repressive Dewey Decimal system. Instead, we went to the IRC, the Instructional Resource Center. The IRC may have had the trappings of the Man's library, but we were free to explore our literary space at our own pace, and we liked it that way.

The cafeteria at Kimpton almost toppled this apple cart of harmonic self-actualization, however. French fries had long been a love/hate thing among students, since the elementary school offerings were usually thick frozen crinkle cut fries barely put through the deep frying process. At Kimpton, however, the cafeteria began to serve thinner shoestring french fries which came ever so close to duplicating the mythical McDonald's fries. The lunch ladies originally served these fries in huge cups, easily double the size of anything served elsewhere. A ritual for eating these fries soon formed. First, the cup would be overturned onto the serving tray. Salt would be added, accompanied by several small paper cups filled with ketchup. This mountain of potatoey goodness would be consumed quickly, lest the small problem of congealing oil spoil the process. That's how it worked for a few weeks, anyway.

As if straight out of a low-budget prison film, however, the polar opposite of self-actualization crept in. The fries became so popular so fast that others who missed out on them the first time would resort to stealing. Swiping someone else's fries became so commonplace that a lot of us would hold a metal fork in one hand while eating our fries with the other. Any inmate who tried to steal our fries ran a serious risk of getting the back of his hand aerated for free. Several students did in fact get stabbed, so the school took measures to curb their criminal impulses. Without admitting any tactical error on its part, the school switched out the metal forks for plastic ones. The stabbings could still take place, but the victory was largely academic. The cafeteria also switched to smaller cups, so the former excesses were no longer a factor.

Another idea borrowed from the Swinging Sixties was the belief that today's dabbler will become tomorrow's customer. Seventh graders were allowed to explore each and every creative or industrial art program for precisely six weeks at a time. This was usually enough time to decide if third degree burns from a spot welder were more to your liking than making (and compelled to eat) cookies made with four TABLESPOONS of baking soda. Students could also decide between a lack of native ability in visual art and a lack of native ability in music. During the eighth grade, enlightened students could choose two of these disciplines for a semester each. After learning how to sew an apron, make a wooden toaster tong, weld coiled wire into a trivet and make a sauce from orange juice and sugar, I opted for the music classes.

One of my music instructors was also a very talented folksinger and guitarist, although local venues were few and far between. We learned the basics of music composition, from scales to notation to rhythm, but I could tell his sweater vest-laden spirit was elsewhere. Every so often, he would break out his acoustic guitar and entertain the class with a passionate rendition of Harry Chapin's ode to absent parenting, "Cat's in the Cradle." He seemed especially wistful during the final verse, in which the son exacts karmic revenge on the inadvertently neglectful narrator/father. I can very easily imagine a major motion picture about his life: "Mr. R's Meaningful Folk Guitar with Hushed, Intimate Vocals Opus."

The other music instructor had a habit of standing in the hallway between classes holding a ukelele and a kazoo. As the young Van Halen and Led Zeppelin fans filed past his classroom door, he would blissfully saw away at a vintage Rudy Vallee or Al Jolson snippet for his own entertainment. Heaven knows WE weren't getting the job done. During class he would throw out challenges to the more musically inclined. One time he asked us all to sing a note as long as we could in a single breath. I remember it came down to me and my church friend and fellow musician Steve S. Steve and I looked at each other as the other competitors dropped out one by one. By the time it was over, Steve and I both looked like the poor opera singer tormented by Bugs Bunny inside the Hollywood Bowl.

Kimpton also provided an intramural sports program for any team members willing to sacrifice a lunch period for the sake of competition. Volleyball was a popular option, followed closely by basketball or dodgeball. The crowd pleasing event, however, was tug-of-war. Almost all of us signed up for at least one session of tug-of-war, especially if it pitted class teams against each other. The rules were fairly straightforward: pull the rope until a centered flag crossed over a designated line. How any team accomplished that goal was strictly up to them. One popular but quasi-legal tactic was to creep forward on the rope whenever any gains were made. This would inevitably lead to one team controlling 99.5 percent of the total rope surface, while 20 other kids desperately held onto the remaining six inches. The other winning strategy was better known as Dean. Dean was one of the biggest guys in our class, and more than willing to share his talent with the rest of the players on his team. The new strategy involve tying one end of the rope around Dean's waist and keeping one hand on the rope for appearance's sake. The tug-of-war intramural battle was clearly for second place during the Dean years.

The two years spent in the welcoming and nuturing arms of educational visionaries like Maslow didn't exactly prepare 8th graders for the next step of the journey. All of us self-actualized little people were about to meet the AntiMaslow, a man named Skinner, in the rat maze and cheese collection known as Workman High School. But that's a story for another day.

WNIR'S DATING SHOW: Gee, And We Had Such Great Expectations, Too.

The local FM talk radio station formerly known as WKNT changed its call letters to WNIR one year, and forever became known to Stowbillies as "Winner 100". The line-up of talk show hosts remained relatively unchanged, with the legendary Howie Chizek keeping most of the heat on during the day. At night, however, the airwaves belonged to a perennially optimistic radio host named Jim Albrecht and his "Dating Show". The Dating Show became 4 hours of the most riveting local radio ever produced, since there was every chance you knew either the caller or the prospective suitors personally. Although the host tried his best to enforce the first names only rule on air, there were always a few callers who inadvertently gave away the identity goods too soon, which in turn led to some serious ribbing at school the next week.

The Dating Show followed a relatively straightforward format. A candidate over the age of 18 would call the WNIR studio number, where he or she might speak with a producer before being put on hold for the actual show. The host would be given a few basic facts—Line 1 is Kerry, 27 years old, from Streetsboro—and he would proceed to chat with her on air for about 10 minutes or so. It was usually enough time for listeners to get the idea that she was a genuine contender and did not reek of desperation and Love's Baby Soft. After Jim and Kerry were through with the first interview, he would open the phone lines to prospective suitors. These callers presumably did NOT go through the same vetting process with a producer that Kerry did. These were often cold calls, with only a 5 second digital delay button standing between them and the general public. Jim would simply answer "Dating show", and the caller would make his pitch. Sometimes the clicking sound we heard was Jim killing out an obscenity-laced rant or adolescent callers who were clearly not in it to win it.

The legitimate callers would undergo one of Jim's patented one minute interrogations, in which he tried to suss out why this caller thought he was good enough to date his "daughter", who was still on hold but could hear everything. If the caller passed the initial sniff test, he would be put on hold while another caller went through the process. Eventually, there would be enough suitors on hold for Kerry to return to the conversation. She would talk to each caller individually, which was indeed every bit as uncomfortable and awkward as it sounds. Jim would then ask Kerry if she was interested in getting to know any of the callers better, and if she actually selected someone (not everyone did), they would exchange phone numbers off the air. This basic pattern continued for 4 more hours: Contestant, chat, callers, interrogation, decision, number exchange. Contestant, chat, callers, interrogation, decision, number exchange.

Because the Dating Show stayed on the air for so many years, it gained a cult following among the locals. We all had Dating Show stories to tell, either as contestants, callers, listeners or critics. The show really became more appealing when many of us migrated to the Kent State or Akron Zoo zip codes and discovered how difficult the adult dating scene could be. Suddenly calling a familiar voice and taking a chance on three strangers while on the radio didn't sound nearly as crazy as it once did. It was certainly no crazier than talking to a punk rock chick over a garbage burger at Jerry's Diner at 3 in the morning, or trying to compete with the Eurotrash dance music offerings at the Town House. At least the mission statement of the Dating show included the idea of actually connecting with someone else who was also at home listening to the radio on a Friday night.

One Dating Show story revolved around a contestant we shall call Denise. Denise was an older woman, with an engaging personality, a strong on-air presence and a somewhat husky voice. Jim chatted with Denise for an unusually long time, which apparently gave Denise the courage to divulge something very personal about her life. At one point, Denise had been a man named Dennis. Dennis apparently had his Little Dennis surgically converted several years earlier, and Denise replaced Dennis on her driver's license. Jim allowed a few seconds of dead air to pass before responding to her with an uncharacteristically tepid "Oh...really?". The mental picture I had in my head was a switchboard filled with blinking lights suddenly going dark. The five second delay button got friction burns as Jim dutifully worked his way through the ineligible callers. Finally a few legitimate calls did get through and he was able to arrange an off-air number exchange between Denise and a man from the progressive city of Akron, Ohio. Jim would later say on air that he had his doubts about Denise and her claims of transsexualism. He became convinced "she" was a male prank caller who wanted to see how far he could go with the character before Jim hung up on him.

A few years later, the station set up a remote broadcast of the Dating Show at a restaurant near Akron. By now, Jim was a local institution, and a lot of former participants wanted to meet him to provide updates or whatever. That night, a woman came up to Jim during a commercial break and introduced herself as Denise. Yes, THAT Denise. She told Jim the date itself didn't work out, but the decision to appear on his show as Denise gave her the confidence to re-enter the dating world as a woman, not as a transvestite. She thanked Jim for treating her with respect, even after the awkward turn their original on air conversation took. Jim mentioned meeting Denise on a later show, noting that she was a very striking woman, and most people would never guess she once had a different set of equipment.

Some of the hook-ups arranged during the show took very bad turns in real life. Most were of the "now some creepy guy has my phone number" variety, but a few were more serious. This is one reason why the host and the producers of the Dating Show encouraged contestants to meet their blind dates at public locations and to use their best judgment when it came to future dates or the sharing of more personal information. The station itself could not be held liable for the actions of contestants or callers, so the show relied heavily on people playing nicely with each other. If things didn't work out after the first date, one person should go this way and the other one should go that way. Two ships and all that.

However, this wasn't always the case, and one night Jim nearly paid the ultimate price for introducing the wrong two people. Apparently the first date did not go well at all, since one of them was *not* a manic depressive psychopath with anger management issues. The other one decided that the Dating Show must pay for putting him together with a woman who did not drink his favorite brand of crazy juice. He called the WNIR studios in search of Jim Albrecht. The message was he was coming to kill him, and Hell was coming with him. Click. The station called several local law enforcement agencies, and they soon had enough information to identify the man and the car he was driving. Because this was all unfolding in real time, listeners would periodically call the station with updates. The car was now in Stow, the car was seen on 59, the car was in downtown Kent, etc. None of this information was of much comfort to Jim, who decided to host the show from underneath his desk that night.

Eventually the man and his car were detained on the road which led to the WNIR studio. The police discovered several empty bottles of alcohol and a loaded revolver in the vehicle. The man continued to issue threats against the Dating Show while being escorted to the Kent city jail. When news of the man's capture reached Jim, he thanked all of his listeners for their support and diligence and resumed his show after a longer than usual commercial break. For those of us listening to the drama unfold over the air, it was a useful object lesson on the hazards of setting up blind dates for a living.

The Dating Show format would eventually lose out to personal ads in tabloid newspapers for singles, then the much wider net of Internet dating websites like Match.com and Great Expectations. More single people wanted to know their potential dates had been professionally vetted, or at least provided legitimate information on their applications and profiles. The randomness and public scrutiny of a call-in radio dating show was no longer as appealing as it had once been, but for a few glorious years in the Stow area, Jim and WNIR did bring a lot of lonely people together, and that can only be a good thing.

WORKMAN HIGH SCHOOL: Nothing a Ramp and Skinner Can't Handle

Practically every major building within the city limits of Stow served some other purpose at some other time in history. The building I knew as Workman High School, the one that serviced primarily 9th and 10th grade students, was at one time Stow High School, the only 9th-12th grade game in town. As Stow's population grew, the original building became hopelessly outgunned by the incoming student bodies. As many of us Stowbillies fondly remember, the city's solution to the problem was to find the best and the brightest architects it could afford, and these skilled men would come up with a solid plan to double the capacity of Stow High School. This scheme would have worked, too, if it hadn't been for those meddling measurements. The new addition was precisely one half-floor higher than the original building. Sorry about that, chief. Missed it by *that* much.

The marriage between old and new sections of Workman was finally achieved with a long, sloping ramp down the middle of a connecting hallway. Few of us missed any opportunity to slide or roll something down that ramp back in the day. The new section also had an elevator, although permission to use said elevator was limited to handicapped students or those who were temporarily out of commission. The rest of us had to choreograph an intricate ballet involving ramps, stairwells, hallways and more hallways. Workman's floor plan was dictated by the educational philosophy championed by Dr. Benjamin Skinner, a leading specialist in draconian teaching methods at the time. Dr. Skinner believed all a student really needed to learn was a desk and a teacher. Like rats in a maze, each student would eventually figure out the optimum way to travel from classroom to classroom. The reward for all of this behavioral conditioning was a quality education with minimal distractions. I would have preferred a lump of cheese myself.

The original part of Workman still featured steam-fed radiators for heat and open windows for non-heat. There was no air conditioning for the comfort of the rat students or their rat instructors. Dr. Skinner would have loved what they did with the place. During the colder months, the steam heat would flow through the cold metal pipes, causing them to expand and contract. This expansion and contraction triggered a series of loud bangs that could be heard throughout the building. It became our two minute warning that heat was finally on the way, one hallway at a time. The new part of Workman also had steam heat, but the architects were clever enough to hide the pipes under more modern covers. We could actually twist knobs that looked like they would have some effect on something. They didn't. Welcome to Ramp World.

One hallway in the original section led to the typing room, where many of us learned how to type on manual typewriters. The instructor would put on a record, and a man who sounded suspiciously like the narrator of every school filmstrip ever would call out letters to type. As we tapped our way through the "A...S...D...F...J...K...L...Sem" assignment over and over again, we had plenty of time to think of the things we'd rather be doing, like not typing endless lines of asdfjkl;. I always thought a sentence like "All work and no play makes Jack a dull boy." would be more interesting, just to see the look on the janitor's face when he emptied out trashcans from The Shining.

Our typing teacher at Workman did find ways to break up the homerow monotony, especially on Friday mornings. She allowed students to bring in their own albums while the rest of us sawed away at assignments printed in a workbook. I'm not sure if she was aware of the artistic leanings of the modern music scene at the time, but she wanted to be hip to the jive and we weren't about to stop her. Because we were so isolated from the rest of the building, volume was not an issue. So those of us who took certain typing courses under a certain typing/English teacher during the early 80s all learned to type while listening to AC/DC's heavy metal album "Back in Black". To this day, I can still hear the clacking of typewriter keys timed to the beat of the title song or "You Shook Me All Night Long".

The library at Workman was not especially spacious, but it was clearly a library, not a Kimptonian instructional resource center. The head librarian was one of those school employees you just knew had been there since brick one of construction. We called her the Mole Lady behind her back, but as deaf as she was, I'm sure we could have bypassed the pretense altogether. The standard procedure for checking out a book from the Workman library was to fill out a card with the student's name and hand it over to the librarian or her assistant for date stamping. This system should have worked well, except for the inevitable Stowbilly factor. A number of students would put a much different name on the card, from Haywood Jablome to Ben Dover. This would usually amount to a whole lot of nothing, since the books would be returned on time anyway and the name used on the card didn't really matter to the circulation assistant.

However, this flaw in the system did backfire spectacularly one day during study hall in the cafeteria. The Mole Lady herself came down from the library, which by Workman hallway standards probably took most of the morning, then approached one of the study hall monitors. She held a book card in one trembling hand, and in her inimitable craggy voice said "Attention, students, attention. We have an overdue book situation. Would Mr. JOHN please report to the library? Mr...ELTON... John?". We were all stunned. We didn't know whether to laugh or cry. She was completely sincere, and completely unaware that Elton John was a British singer-songwriter who had graduated years ago. Finally, someone shouted from the back of the room: "Elton's not here today, ma'am. He's on tour with Peter Frampton." Without missing a beat, the Mole Lady said "Well, would you please tell Mr. John to see me in the library when he gets back? It's very important that I speak with him." And then she was gone.

The original section of Workman was clearly built during a different time than my own. There were secrets around every corner, and most of them were inspired by the Red Menace scare of the 1950s. The small gym in the basement, which my predecessors often used as a makeshift dance hall during lunch, also served as an official atomic bomb shelter. A storage room connected to the gym still contained the remnants of emergency food supplies from the 1950s. There was also a tunnel which led from that storage room to the basement of the City Hall building. The City Hall building also had the iconic Civil Defense Shelter signs from the blissful "Duck and Cover" days. Considering the size of the student population at Workman and the capacity of the underground gym and bunker, there may have been a discussion or two in the day about who would get to enjoy the emergency rations and who would be toast during an actual atomic event.

The newer section of Workman housed many of the science classrooms, which meant access to Bunsen burners and a few serious chemicals. One of my favorite biology teachers was also an amateur bodybuilder, so his class lectures would often include the phrase "getting huge", followed by a Schwarzenegger-inspired pose or two. He would also perform experiments which were clearly not sanctioned by the school, but were usually fun to watch. One experiment involved pouring two liquid compounds together in a very tall glass cylinder. Nothing happened for a few minutes, but he explained that some chemicals generate significant heat when combined and we should just keep watching. A minute later, a steaming hot foam rose from the top of the cylinder, spilled over the side and flowed over the desk. The foam continued to slide along the floor and then out the classroom door.

What we may have called an exothermic reaction on the test soon became a smoldering pile of goo in the hallway.

The restrooms at Workman varied in overall quality and usability. The showers in the locker rooms were legendarily bad, followed closely by the student restrooms by the north entrance. In an effort to thwart smokers, the doors to each stall had been removed, which was not as much of a deal breaker on the boys' side as it was for the girls' side. Our assistant principal would periodically receive reports of illicit smoking in the girls room and throw a bucket of water through the front entrance. His actual smoker to poor girl just trying to brush her hair before class ratio was pretty abysmal, however. Other restrooms were much better, and the ones in the teachers' lounges were the best of all. This may explain why so many teachers went into apoplectic fits whenever a student wandered into the lounge by mistake. They were zealously protecting their pristine bathroom stalls, replete with working doors and abundant ashtrays.

They say all barely adequate but legally sufficient things must pass, and the Workman building was no exception. After the new 9th through 12th grade Stow-Munroe Falls High School became operational during the late 80s, the Workman building was generally abandoned. It would eventually be torn down, and the land would be converted for retail use. Many young Stowites would never guess an entire high school once stood on the property where Marc's is today. Many older Stowbillies, however, still remember running laps around the field behind the building, walking down to the public library after school, or hanging out at Eddie's bike shop or the Lawson's parking lot. The Workman building (and its surprisingly good cafeteria) may be gone, but many of us will miss that old Skinner box and its promise of better cheese to come.

Silence of the Chipped Chopped Hams: Legendary Foods Every Stowbilly Remembers

Growing up in Stow meant developing a taste for cheap cold cuts, especially those containing the word "loaf." Grocery stores like Acme Click and Reinker's had deli departments with the usual selections of ham, roast beef and turkey, but it rarely stopped there. Those meats lived on the right side of the sliced meat tracks, but were usually too expensive for our school lunch bags or Dad's lunchbox. The working class cold cuts lived on the poorly lit side of the deli case. Their names were Dutch loaf, ham loaf, pickle loaf and the dreaded olive loaf. Many of us still remember going to school with little brown bags filled with a Dutch loaf sandwich on white bread, a postage stamp sized bag of corn chips and an apple. My mother would occasionally spread a thin layer of margarine across the bread before applying the mayonnaise, apparently in an effort to keep the bread from becoming soggy. It really only converted an already questionable sandwich into a not-quite-butter flavored questionable sandwich.

The loaf meats became a staple in many Stowbilly households, but the *capo de capo* of inexpensive lunch meats had to be a processed ham loaf chipped off the slicer as thinly as possible. This was, of course, chipped chopped ham (or chip chop, if you lived at my house). Chipped chopped ham was noticeably less expensive than its more accomplished honey or smoked ham brethren. This amalgamation, formed and pressed from different ham sources, was then placed on a special slicer capable of making exceptionally thin cuts while the loaf was slammed repeatedly against the blade. The result was a remarkably flavorful cold cut which was more art than science. A huge mound of chipped chopped ham from Isaly's or Click would only set the family back a dollar or so, and it was awesome when pan fried with barbecue sauce or ketchup. Fresh white bread was the only logical choice for a sandwich accompaniment in our household.

For the younger Stowbilly on the move, interested in looking cool at any cost, a toothpick was an essential tool, and the flavor of the day was cinnamon; the hotter, the better. Several drugstores sold an array of flavored oils, from spearmint to citrus to cotton candy. By far the most popular flavor among those in the know was cinnamon. The thing to do was buy a box of wooden toothpicks and a bottle of cinnamon oil, then soak a supply of toothpicks in the cinnamon oil bottle for at least 24 hours—longer if you were in sadomasochism or self-immolation. These hot toothpicks could be brought to school legally, since they were clearly not chewing or bubble gum. Chewing on an especially pickled cinnamon toothpick became a rite of passage for some of us.

The other cinnamon-based product many of us carried to school were miniature jawbreakers known as Atomic Fireballs. As with the chipped chopped ham, Isaly's became a popular source for these individually wrapped balls of fire. A kid could buy a substantial amount of Atomic Fireballs for a quarter at Isaly's, then resell them at a profit during regular school hours. They became a form of sugar-laden currency, and any 6th grade boy packing some serious Atomic Fireball heat became the man other men wanted to be, and all the women wanted to be with. No, seriously. I mean it.

Pizza was another hot commodity in Stow, and there were some legendary rivalries between suppliers. Altieri's had the hometown advantage, since just about everyone in town knew anyone who had ever owned the place. Parasson's had the field advantage, since it was situated on the same street as the original high school. Bella Vista had it for authenticity, since very few people outside of Italy itself could have possibly been as Italian as the brothers who operated it. My personal favorite, however, was Angelina's, which had no tactical advantage whatsoever. It was situated in a wedge between two streets, and patrons had to climb several concrete steps to even reach the front door. Angelina's pizza oven ran so hot that it routinely burned the toppings to a pleasant crisp. This was a plus in my book.

Parasson's was a memorable dining venue all by itself. Early in its history, the building was used as an inn and also a restaurant that introduced the idea of an all-inclusive smorgasbord to our humble little burg (for non-Midwesterners, an all-inclusive smorgasbord is another term for an all-you-can eat buffet). When it became an Italian restaurant, the owners took advantage of the floor plan and converted each room into themed dining areas: English Tudor, Italian, garden greenhouse and so on. Regulars would know to ask the hostess for a specific room, but those outside the loop would usually end up in the glass-enclosed greenhouse room in the middle of August. Nothing on the menu was better than the dark rumor that passed from generation to generation, however. The claim was that the building also served as a funeral home before it became a family-friendly Italian restaurant. The word on the street was that several former restaurant employees had been dispatched to the basement for supplies and discovered: A) A secret room used for embalming bodies. B) The remains of an oven used for cremations. or C) An elevator used to transport caskets to the viewing rooms above.

The other food-related rivalry that many Stowbillies experienced first-hand involved ice cream and ice cream novelties. Isaly's built its reputation on the quality of its hard-packed ice cream, which would be dipped out of a coffin freezer and pressed into a sugar cone or one of those styrofoamesque cones with an internal support structure Frank Lloyd Wright would have admired. For those who preferred their ice cream with some chew and moral heft, Isaly's was clearly the way to go. Isaly's ran a small short-order diner in the back area, and milkshakes or sundaes made from one of 20-plus flavors were very popular.

Close to Isaly's was another ice cream joint that was so nice they named it at least twice. When I was very young, during the early 70s, the place was called PDQ, short for Pretty Darn Quick. I wouldn't know; I just sat in the car. I remember there was an eggnog-flavored powdered milk additive also called PDQ, so I would order an eggnog milkshake from PDQ. PDQ changed hands and became Stow Cone. Stow Cone kept up many of the traditions established by PDQ, and was especially popular after school sporting events. The back of the parking lot also happened to be the top of an impressive natural gorge, however, so making that left turn out of the drive-through lane was always a good decision.

Although not technically within the city limits, for many of us, the final word on all things ice cream was found at a frozen custard stand called Stoddard's. Stoddard's did not serve that simple peasant dish known as ice cream. No, it served frozen custard—the dairy product our mothers warned us about. Frozen custard had a much higher percentage of butterfat than regular ice cream, and the machines' agitators turned twice as slowly, which meant far less air in the final product. Quite fairly, frozen custard stands have been described as the places where God gets His ice cream. Stoddard's was definitely one of our local houses of worship. A single scoop of Stoddard's frozen custard cost 25 cents at one point, but woe unto the child who had to stop short for traffic and watch his beloved custard fall off the cone and onto the ground.

Because frozen custard was a labor-intensive process and they only owned three machines, Stoddard's only produced three flavors at a time: Vanilla, Chocolate and the Flavor of the Day. The vanilla was awesome, the chocolate was powerfully good, but the flavor of the day was always a crap shoot. Some days it would be something amazingly good, like banana or strawberry or blueberry, while other days it would be something not so tempting, like pineapple or butterscotch or mint chocolate chip. A small sign near the roadside announced the flavor of the day, and I would adjust my stride according to the selection. If it was blueberry, dead sprint. If it was pineapple, slow crawl. If it was mint chocolate chip, my least favorite at the time, tactical retreat. Stoddard's was a ritual for those of us who attended the Apostolic Pentecostal church 200 yards away, as well as for those who happened to live in a house 210 yards away.

There were a lot of other foodstuffs from that time many of us Stowbillies still crave to this day. Lawson's was a convenience store chain with locations spaced out about every hundred yards or so. One of its most popular products was a French onion dip so good that people simply dropped every extraneous word to describe it. It was simply Lawson's Chip Dip. Nothing tasted better on a wavy potato chip or a Doritos tortilla chip (or for that matter, cardboard), than Lawson's Chip Dip. When Lawson's franchises began to disappear from the landscape, the new convenience store chains made every effort to keep that same French Onion dip stocked on their shelves.

My mother used to make a comfort food she called tuna macaroni salad, and one ingredient became so popular that it was often used in place of the term "salad dressing" in church cookbooks. Cooks did not add two cups of salad dressing to anything; they added Spin Blend. Spin Blend was a zippy little number with a distinctive green lid and attitude to burn. The official list of ingredients only mentioned lemon juice and vinegar, but we all knew in our Stowbilly hearts that here there be horseradish. Spin Blend turned an ordinary cold pasta salad into an explosion of Pennsylvania Dutch-inspired madness. Spin Blend could even turn a Dutch loaf or chipped chopped ham sandwich into one of the best sandwiches any kid ever put in his lunch bag, even with that obscene swath of greasy margarine standing between the meat and the aptly-named Wonder bread.

There are many other favorite Stowbilly foods and beverages that did not get mentioned in this essay, but trust me they will get their day in the sun in future issues. I'm thinking about Wacky Packs, Sto-nut donuts, JoJo potato wedges, burgers at the Flagpole, and whatever pickled thing was in that jar on the counter at Eddie's. No journey would be complete without trips to the Red Barn, Rax, Around the

Clock and Osman's Pies, either. Stay tuned. There's a lot more nostalgia where this came from.

LAKEVIEW HIGH SCHOOL: Incidentally, No Lake and No View.

Somewhere between Kimpton's wild 60s architectural excesses and Workman's staple-as-you-go utilitarianism was Lakeview High School, the final 2 in Stow's clearly improvised 2-2-2 higher education plan.

When Workman ceased to be workable as Stow's sole 9-12th grade high school, Lakeview became the "new" high school, thoughtfully located a quarter of a mile away from the existing one. There are those who still recall the day when the first class scheduled to graduate from Lakeview made its historic trek from Workman to the Lakeview campus. As the school yearbook would document, these pioneers weren't about to let a construction fence get in the way of educational progress, no sir.

Some of us Workmanites first experienced Lakeview as members of the marching band. Those freshmen and sophomore students would get off the buses at Lakeview and assemble on the practice field while the rest of us rode an additional quarter of a mile to Workman. Following band practice, there would be a parade of young band members walking to the Workman campus, while others made their way up to Lakeview for drivers' education classes. That walk between Lakeview and Workman could either be a welcome break from the Skinner box or an object lesson on why others leave NE Ohio in droves during winter months. Since the class times did not always take into account the commute between campuses, most of us developed a walking pace somewhere between deliberate and alarmingly laser-focused.

Lakeview also featured a parking lot for both students and faculty, a situation which naturally cried out for a sense of law and order. The responsibilities of this position fell on one man and one man only, and that man had a name: One Bullet Barney, aka Rent-a-Cop. Barney indeed took his job very seriously, even if the driving student population did not. Getting past the Rent-a-Cop was the first step in a multi-step plan to get to McDonald's and back during the lunch period. The final step was getting back on campus while Barney was distracted by other student drivers working on step one. Getting a citation from Barney usually carried about as much weight as getting an overdue book notice from the Mole Lady at Workman, but few Stowbillies wanted to stay on his bad side for very long. He had a long memory, and a few friends still on the force.

Although the parking lot situation could be troubling at times, it paled in comparison to the vandalism magnet we euphemistically called the courtyard. The courtyard's centralized location and restricted access seriously harshed its buzz as a functional space, but it still served a purpose for senior classes during the last weeks of school. The aforementioned McDonald's restaurant had one thing every senior class hoped to capture, but only a handful ever did. Once every few years, a clearly disgruntled maintenance staff would have to fish a large fiberglass horse out of the courtyard, the same statue usually found in front of the Golden Arches of Stow. Sometimes a few crudities would be "painted" with bleach on the vulnerable courtyard grass, while at other times very large items would be dismantled and reassembled in the courtyard's confined space. If it was large and missing within five miles of Stow (especially during late May), searching in Lakeview's courtyard would not have been a bad idea.

Much like Kimpton's bucket of french fries or Workman's revered peanut butter bars, Lakeview's cafeteria had one feature that kept the faithful coming back for more. The standard lunch was generally satisfying, but for only an additional quarter students could stand in line for what was promoted as a chocolate milkshake. In retrospect, the fact that the milkshake mix was provided by the spoilsports at the USDA should have been a clue. It may not have been on a par with Friendly's or Stoddard's, but at least it was cold and creamy. Chocolaty, however, it was not. Nevertheless, many of us with two bits burning a hole in our pockets would dutifully stand in line all lunch period for a shot at natural dairy product goodness. The milkshake line also featured a few other snack items generally not found on the standard lunch menu, such as potato chips and candy bars. It was an alternative nation, a wink and a nod to nutritional mutiny in a lunchroom dedicated to the vagaries of the subsidized lunch program.

Lakeview during the early 80s was the site of a few other social experiments, like the ill-fated attempt to change the school's colors to pink and black and adopt a new mascot: The Stow High Good and Plentys. There were plenty of valid signatures on that petition, but unfortunately decades of maroon and gold tradition did not play in our favor. Another science project could be described as "one milk carton, one unused locker". After several months, the consensus among us scientists was that milk cartons were incredibly resilient, but things could only continue in one unfortunate direction. An unwashed gym shirt we named Fred Bread was also left in an unused locker for several months, but that experiment ended during a surprise locker inspection, which yielded a few illegal substances, some Playboy magazines and a green, fuzz-covered gym shirt. Fred Bread taught us a lot about living, about dying, and what it was to be a man. Actually, he taught us the value of a roll of quarters and a cup of laundry detergent.

One positive thing about the Lakeview campus was there was everything in a room and a room for everything. The building itself was almost a military-industrial complex in scope, with metal and wood shops, a massive gymnasium and locker rooms, band and choir rooms, business school rooms for IOE students, a darkroom for yearbook and newspaper photographers, not to mention offices for teachers and classrooms for everything from Latin to physics. The only catch was that students had five minutes at best to travel between all of those areas. Logistics rarely entered the equation whenever we were selecting our classes for the next semester. Anyone who signed up for Algebra II and choir, for example, would have to run from the last room of the top floor on the north side of the building to one of the last rooms on the bottom floor of the south side. The first bell served two purposes: the end of the class period, and the start of the daily 300 yard dash to the gym's locker room.

One class at Lakeview became very popular because of Ohio state law. A would-be driver under the age of 18 was required by law to present a certificate of completion from a recognized driver's ed school. Those who could afford the tuition fees had the option of attending what we liked to call a "crash course" on driving. Sear's offered a four day driver's ed course that satisfied at least the spirit of the law. Successful students would indeed receive a certificate of completion and could take their driving test in Cuyahoga Falls. However, there were many of us who enjoyed turning that kind of privileged positive into a Stowbilly negative. If a driver in the Stow area ever did something hazardous, like stopping short or failing to signal a turn, many of us would yell "Where did you learn to drive? SEARS?".

Meanwhile, the rest of us who were of driving age would sign up for the school-sponsored driver's ed course at Lakeview. This meant 18 weeks of classroom, simulator and real world training, but at least we wouldn't drive like those heathens with the Cracker Jack box certificates. The driver's ed instructor had exactly the demeanor you would expect from a social studies teacher shanghaied into teaching 16 years how to handle a 3,000 pound Deathmobile. He was fond of pointing out that he was a fervent bicyclist, so he was essentially giving us the means and ability to run him off the road later. We would watch the required "Blood Runs Red on the Highway" snuff films, spend time behind the wheel of a 1963 Studebaker in a driving simulator, then drive around town in a real car. The instructor did have a second brake installed on his side, however. At the end of the course, he doled out the certificates of completion, which he called "death certificates", and warned us all not to say anything approaching a thank you.

I'll end with one final memory of a teacher from Lakeview, a man who fought in Korea and enjoyed repeating his one good story about the place. It seems he was a hit with the local ladies because of his thick red hair, and they gave him a Korean nickname which he translated as "Number One Redhead". He taught history at Lakeview, although he was the kind of person I always thought should be *making* history somewhere else. I really enjoyed his class, and sometimes I would visit him during my 8th period study hall. He also owned a miniature golf course, so occasionally he would hand me a set of free passes to play a game or two. One day I walked into his empty classroom and found him watching TV. It wasn't a standard over-the-air channel, but an uncut cable movie channel. The cable television line ran on a pole right outside his classroom window, so he managed to splice some coaxial cable and tap into the signal. We watched Superman II for an entire class period, then I left to catch my bus. That's one of my lasting memories from my time spent at Lakeview High School, the building with no lake and no view, but still plenty of heart and soul.

EXTREMELY LATE NIGHT TELEVISION: The Revolution WILL Be Televised, at 2:30 In The Morning.

Most Stowbilly children, especially teenagers, knew that the really good stuff didn't show up on TV until at least 11:30 on a Friday night. That's when Channel 8 in Cleveland handed over the reins to a weatherman and a broadcast engineer, AKA Hoolihan and Big Chuck. Hoolihan and Big Chuck's show was an amalgamation of schlocky horror movies, song parodies, Certain Ethnic jokes and sketch comedy clearly filmed on the cheap with someone else's equipment. It was pure camp, but we watched every last minute of it, all the way to the last segment where Hoolihan and Big Chuck, dressed in tacky animal print pajamas, would read jokes submitted by their loyal viewers. We needed to hear these jokes, because we would inevitably be retelling them at school on Monday morning. By the end of the broadcast, we would be too exhausted to move from the couch to the TV set, so we just let it run. We...just...let...it...run.

The end of Hoolihan and Big Chuck may have signaled the final gasp of local programming, but it was not the end of late night television as we knew it. Our sleep-deprived Midwestern minds could still be blown by the rock concerts featured on another channel. It may have been Don Kirschner's Rock Concert or The Midnight Special, like any of us could tell the difference at 1 in the morning. Whichever show it was, Cousin It and the Cousin It Band were usually getting down with their bad selves on a smoke-filled stage. All I remember is that they were scary to watch, but clearly devoted to their craft. They may have been the Allman Brothers, they may have been Blue Oyster Cult, they may have even been the Doobie Brothers or Foghat, but whatever it was, it was clearly a taste of music from the land of cool people. It's just too bad we weren't nearly awake enough to let sonic art wash over us.

For those of us whose parents did not believe in the beauty of cable television, another late night music show became our own version of MTV. NBC would show two hours of last year's hottest videos, but we didn't care. We got to see Adam Ant and Cyndi Lauper and Talking Heads and...well, those other guys with the hair. I think they had synthesizers, but don't quote me on that. While The Midnight Special and Rock Concert may have an abundance of soul, the late night video show on NBC had the promise of a Madonna-like product, sir. Life for a bleary-eyed Stowbilly boy became much better as soon as he learned a Go-Go or Bangle or Benatar would play a significant role in it. With the arrival of home VCRs, the late night music video show became one of the first things we learned to program on the timer.

Meanwhile, the comedy was still going strong on other channels, even if it took a turn to the left. If Saturday Night Live was the best American late night sketch comedy of its day, then SCTV was its hipper Canadian cousin. The cast of SCTV read like a Who's Who of comedy, from John Candy to Rick Moranis to Eugene Levy, with stops in-between for Martin Short, Andrea Martin, Joe Flaherty and Catherine O'Hara. SCTV, which stood for Second City Television, had the luxury of taping their segments over time, but they still maintained a sense of immediacy like Saturday Night Live. Characters like Doug and Bob McKenzie, horror show host Count Floyd and the Five Neat Guys became the stuff of legend. If another kid at school quoted the Farm Film Report ("he blowed up. He blowed up REAL good), then you knew he was hip to the same late night jive. It was one thing to stay up until the pajama jokes on Hoolihan and Big Chuck, but something else entirely if you stayed up until the end credits of SCTV. There were many Sunday mornings when devoted SCTVers would drag themselves to church or simply call in sick and sleep until noon.

There were other shows on network television that would have clearly been out of place at any other time. Some of us still remember the Uncle Floyd show, which was undoubtedly the strangest half-hour of the night. Uncle Floyd, as some of us discovered later, worked the same alternative comedy venues as Paul Reubens, aka Pee Wee Herman. His show could loosely be described as a talk show, although his guests were not generally known for their conversational skills, and his personal sidekick spent the entire show in a catatonic stupor. What made the Uncle Floyd show so entertaining was the fact that it just showed up at 2 or 3 in the morning, and was never actually listed in the local TV guide. This turned an otherwise *avant garde* comedy show into a "how did *this* show get a time slot?" subversive act of programming. Occasionally, the original Pee Wee Herman show, which should never be mistaken for the sanitized CBS version, would also show up on extremely late night television. Pee Wee's show often showcased the alternative, edgy, dark comedians and performers our parents should have warned us about. Yes, there really was a band called the Plasmatics. Yes, there really was a 2:30 in the morning. No, the Plasmatics and 2:30 in the morning shouldn't be in the same sentence when you're 12 years old and hopped up on Doritos and cheap soda.

Whenever extremely late night network television would fail us, there was always the audiovisual toss-up known as UHF. If the local UHF channels, like WUAB-13 or channel 61, hadn't already called it a night, they would usually show grade Z horror movies, like Attack of the Wasp Woman or The Flesh Eaters. I'm saying it now, this was a miscalculation of epic proportions. The Flesh Eaters' plot revolved around a group of very unpleasant people who survived a plane crash and were now trapped on a deserted island. Unbeknownst to them, but plenty beknownst to the 12 year old audience, they were also surrounded by alien flesh-eating bacteria. One unprotected step into the water and it would be a bubbly, fluorescent kind of death for someone. The only member of the cast I was hoping would go flesh eater-free was the plane's pilot, who reminded me of the guy who *should* have gotten the role of the Professor on Gilligan's Island. As it turned out, he did indeed escape the island, after figuring out a way to electrocute the little alien buggers in bulk. Creepy, creepy movie.

The other UHF channels held their own after-hours charm, including the public television station that decided to broadcast the next day's object lessons during the wee smalls. At three in the morning, even first grade math was a challenge. Another UHF channel, clearly from a distant location, showed fuzzy reruns of shows like Mr. Ed and The Munsters, two shows that are far too high concept at three in the morning. The freakiest opening credit of a television show ever has got to be the creepy marionette Lucille Ball dancing her way through "Here's Lucy!". Wrong, wrong, wrong.

One dirty little secret about UHF channels and the Stowbilly boys who watched them is about to be revealed. One UHF channel decided to dip its toe in the paid television market, which would include adult movies with adult content. Their plan was to scramble their signal at a certain time at night, then offer descrambling devices to paid subscribers. OUR plan, however, was to hope the engineer in charge of scrambling the signal would either shirk his duties or call in sick. The scrambled signal would be vaguely watchable, if a wavy, soundless negative of a picture could be defined as "watchable". We didn't care, as long as we could see flashes of wavy, negative breasts on an actress with black teeth. The station insisted on showing cheaply produced European sex comedies from the 1970s, most of which were based on familiar fairy tales. The experiment didn't last more than a few years, but during that time many of us received an incomplete education that would require years of careful descrambling.

ESSAYS FROM "The Lost StoryHouse Coffee Essays" collection

GOING BOTTOMLESS

I believe all those who call themselves serious coffee drinkers should go bottomless as often as possible. While your neurons try desperately to erase that imagery, allow me to explain. Before this country became one giant parking lot for Starbucks, we had diners, roadside grills, greasy spoons, holes in the wall, mom and pop stands, donut shops, burger joints, and other examples of American gastronomic superiority. All of these establishments had one thing in common- the patented Bottomless Cup of Coffee. For a few measly quarters, one could enjoy an endless supply of industrial strength motor oil coffee, refilled at critical moments by sympathetic hands.

Going bottomless is not for the faint of heart- it's a lifestyle choice that demands a lot of dedication from its practitioners. If you go bottomless, be prepared to have an opinion on everything, from national politics to what's wrong with these kids today. Bottomless coffee isn't served by 18 year old college freshmen named Brittany or Kelli- it's flung out by waitresses named Edna or Polly or Eunice. These angels in comfortable shoes have already been there, already done that, and have strapped on the apron to prove it. When you go bottomless long enough, the fourth wall between waitress and customer comes down with a satisfying thud.

The entire Bottomless Cup industry hinges on ritual. The first cup- only a warm-up swing, a little loosening of the pipes. The second cup comes around and suddenly the world is a much nicer place. Now is a great time to fling out the best thought on your mind- just get it on the table and see who runs with it. By the time cup three rolls around, you notice that Edna looks a little tired. The debate over Ginger or Mary

Ann is still raging strong, though, so now's not the time to pry. Cup four is usually the deal-breaker, unless you have a hollow leg. Mary Ann is leading by a wide enough margin for you to make a dignified exit. You make your goodbyes, pat Edna platonically on the arm and slip her an extra dollar for her troubles. Another Bottomless day is complete.

Now go out there and grab yourself a bottomless cup o' Joe, for old time's sake. Oh yeah- and tell Edna I sure do miss her cooking.

TENK YOU, BOYZA!

You don't have to be Norwegian to understand Lawrence Welk, but apparently it helps. The other night I had my trusty mug of coffee in one hand and the tv remote in the other, scanning the channels man-style for something to watch. You know what man-style channel surfing is like- give each channel exactly three nanoseconds to prove itself worthy of a stop. Sad to say, partial nudity does play a part in the decision-making process.

I took a few sips of strong, dark courage and eventually settled on the red-headed stepchild of the free broadcast world- PBS. In defense of public television, may I say how fun it would be to watch a show like Fear Factor have to beg for every nickel it needs, while the Antiques Roadshow gets a million dollars per episode. But I digress.

There on my screen stands bandleader Lawrence Welk, fronting a band outfitted in what can only be described as early Paintshop Explosionwear. I understand that color television was a new and wondrous thing in Welk's day, but couldn't they have limited the clothing scheme to colors that exist in nature? I managed to catch some episodes from the early 60s, and I must say the boys looked mighty sharp in their tailored, thin-lapeled suits with the Cuban boots. Then all of a sudden the spirit of good taste and restraint passed right over the studio door. The result was a collision between a Day-Glo paint truck and a circus train.

Even more disconcerting than the clothes were the performers themselves. I had no idea you could actually airbrush a live human being. Maybe it was the coffee talking, but I started to feel like I had tripped into the Stepford Wives Comedy Variety Hour by mistake. All that was missing was a surprise appearance by the Pointer Sisters and the comedic stylings of Mr. David Brenner.

You know, it's a funny thing about nostalgia. Dylan might have been onto something when he said 'what looks large from a distance/ Close up ain't never that big', but when it comes to the Lawrence Welk show and all of its apparent corniness, perhaps it's we who have gotten smaller somehow. Enna one, enna two...

KAFFEEKLATSCHES, AND THE PEOPLE WHO LOVE THEM

As I began writing this essay, the news of Ann Lander's passing had just arrived. This unfortunate turn of events got me to thinking about our collective need for solid advice, and the lengths we are willing to go in order to find it.

For many of us, advice has become a double-edged sword. We want to hand it out freely, but painful experience has taught us that most people don't want it. We've resorted to asking for permission, which to me is just one notch below signing a legal waiver: "Do you swear or affirm that the advice you are about to issue will not in any way cause irreparable harm to the recipient, (insert name here)?" Sign here, and here, and initial there, please. Thank you. So, do you think I should invite him to the wedding?

Of course, the original and best source for advice continues to be the kaffeeklatsch. There is no problem large enough to stump 12 middle-aged women armed with strong coffee and blueberry danishes. Solutions will come flying out fast and furious, and cover everything from Barbara's divorce to Sue's bursitis to the inherent shortcomings of the Monroe Doctrine. If you really want a problem solved and solved right, find your local Klatsch representative and just let the magic happen. Word to the wise- poundcake.

I admire anyone who can give advice year after year and not lose every friend they own. Ann Landers did that for over 40 years and did it well. I hope she's sitting in a Heavenly Kaffeeklatsch right now, sipping gourmet coffee and answering some very interesting mail: "Dear Ann, What if I was all wrong about that gravity thing? Do you think anyone will notice? Isaac N., England". "Dear Ann, I'm having a party for all of my royal subjects. Should I serve punch or just let them eat cake? Marie A., France". One thing's for sure, Ann Landers will never run out of things to do.

FINDING YOUR INNER NUGE

A few years ago, I read an article exhorting readers to find their inner Ted Nugent. By that I gathered we should all embrace our inner gun-toting, caveman-thinking, Alpha-male tendencies once in a while. Oh yeah, and while we're at it we should learn three chords on a really loud guitar and play the same four songs until we die and/or retire. I have a sinking feeling the Nuge would have earned the title "Motorcity Madman" whether he was a rock star or a third-shift busboy at Denny's.

Since I have no interest in acquiring cat scratch fever, I have acquired a new hero. I want to get in touch with my inner Kaldi. For those of you who may be unfamiliar with the history of coffee, Kaldi is the fun-loving Abysinnian goat-herder responsible for discovering an elixir we now call coffee. Legend has it that Kaldi was leading some of his charges through a neighbor's field when they came upon a bush bristling with red berries. The sheep began eating these berries in earnest. Kaldi noticed that his sheep began dancing like frat boys on prom night. Never one to pass up an opportunity to ingest something unproven and potentially life-threatening, Kaldi sampled a few berries himself and became the prototype for SBC customers everywhere. He later shared his discovery with some local monks, who refined the process and produced a bitter but drinkable beverage. They noticed that a few sips of this concoction would give them the ability to stay awake during prayers. Ironically enough, a thousand years later we would be drinking the stuff to stay awake through everything else.

The story of Kaldi, Abyssinian ambassador of strong coffee and dancing sheep, may be apocryphal, but I'd still like to glean a few nuggets of wisdom from it anyway. Sometimes in life you just have to take the word of your flock and throw a few red berries down your gullet. Maybe you'll discover a new and exciting beverage for the ages, or maybe you'll discover a new paint thinner. Maybe you'll discover a new beverage AND a paint thinner, who knows? What doesn't kill you just makes you stronger, or at least more awake in church. So raise a mug to the spirit of Kaldi, a man who missed his calling as a kamikaze pilot or rock guitar legend. As for me, I'll have what the sheep are having, thank you very much.

THE COFFEE BEAN THAT TIME AND STARBUCKS FORGOT

A moment of silence please, for the coffee bean that time forgot. (......) Thank you. Now I'll tell you the story about *coffea stenophylla* and why it's not sitting in your cup as we speak. There are at least 25 species of plant belonging to the *Coffea* family, but only a handful make up the bulk of commercially produced coffee. The most familiar is *arabica*, considered to be the best bean for gourmet coffee roasting. Arabica beans account for a full 75% of the world's commercial production of coffee. The rest of the market consists primarily of *robusta* and *liberica* beans, which are easier to grow than *arabica* but are not especially flavorful. You'll most likely run into *robusta* beans in the budget coffee aisle or in instant blends. Truth be told, you'll probably find *liberica* beans sitting on a dock somewhere, accompanied by an exasperated coffee broker moaning about his lot in life.

But the dominance of the arabica bean was not always a done deal. In the mid-1890s, a variety of coffee named *coffea stenophylla* was discovered in West Africa and brought to the attention of several English coffee plantation owners. Stenophylla was said to be more flavorful than arabica, and even more resistant to the leaf rust problem that devastated most of the plantations. On the surface, stenophylla appeared to be the ideal solution for plantation owners desperate to replace their ruined crops. But it was this same desperation that proved to be the death knell for *coffea stenophylla*. The one major difference between stenophylla and arabica was the growing time. Stenophylla took 9 years to mature into a high-yielding plant, while arabica trees grew to maturity in 7 years or less. Plantation owners chose to cultivate the arabica variety of coffee for strictly economic reasons. Stenophylla soon fell out of favor as a commercially viable crop, and today is primarily grown in Guinea and the Ivory Coast. Some say it has a flavor closer to tea, which probably doesn't do it many favors in the demanding field of coffee cultivation. To my way of thinking, *coffea stenophylla* will always be the fifth Beatle of the gourmet coffee world-it came ever so close to the Big Show, but time and fate had other ideas.

SO WHAT HAVE *YOU* BEEN DOING?

As I take a few reflective sips of coffee this morning, I'm reminded of an impending personal milestone. For reasons which will soon become apparent, I'm tempted to change that to read 'personal MILLstone'.

Next year will mark my twentieth season out of high school. Of course you realize this means plane tickets, ill-fitting suits, complete memory loss, hotel reservations and an open bar. Guess which one will get my fullest attention. It's not that I'm against the need for class reunions on some intellectual plane, but sometimes I question the wholesale marketing of what may be a rather painful yardstick for some. I anticipate receiving quite a few unsolicited invitations from companies who specialize in class reunions. I have a feeling I'm going to separating a little wheat from a boatload of chaff when January arrives.

At first I feared that no one from my class would even find me. I just knew I'd end up on that collective Wanted Poster you always see in the local newspaper. Now with the glories of the Internet in full bloom, my new fear is that EVERYONE will find me. I can't speak for all of you, but don't you sometimes think of your former classmates as perpetual teenagers? My last contact with 90% of my class was in the years of Reaganomics and fluorescent clothing. I'm not sure I'm ready to meet the modern editions who will show up en masse at the one country club in my hometown. I just know I'm going to expect parachute pants and leg warmers a-plenty, while the DJ plays Duran Duran and a Flock of Seagulls. As badly as I want to meet the accountants, teachers, housewives and small business owners of today, part of me still wants to crawl back into the 80s womb and talk about Luke and Laura's wedding all night. Nostalgia isn't everything, but sometimes it's the thing that will keep you the warmest.

"YOU SHOULD REALLY TRY OUT FOR THE OLYMPICS, KID."

I hold coffee, Andy Coiner and Calvin Rydbom partially responsible for my short-lived life of crime- coffee, because it was 20 degrees that night, with a windchill factor of liquid nitrogen, Andy Coiner, because he was just plain *wrong*, and Calvin Rybom, because he was in the wrong bleacher at exactly the wrong time.

Andy Coiner was a buddy of mine who lived in the city adjoining my hometown. Our schools were notorious football rivals- some of the old-school Cleveland Browns came from these two institutions. Andy was a natural athlete- strong, wiry and basically fearless. In contrast, I was a thinker, not a fighter. Nonetheless, our two teams were playing on the official Coldest Night of the Year. That's where the first leg of the problem started- artificial coffee courage. Andy had a plan.

My brother and I followed Andy through the woods and right up to a large fence surrounding the football stadium. Time for the second leg of the problem- Andy's amazing climbing ability. He shimmied up and over the fence, followed quickly by my brother. I was the last of the Hole in the Head gang left. Enter Calvin Rydbom. It just so happened that the fence was located on the visitors side of things—in other words, MY school's section. Calvin happened to be on the highest bleacher, which meant he had a perfect view of our crime scene. As I struggled in vain to scale the fence, Calvin decided to encourage me in his own fashion. By the time I reached the top, the entire bleacher section was cheering me on. I fell over the fence and landed at the feet of an off-duty police officer. He escorted me to the ticket office, after congratulating me on my Olympic fence-climbing style. My days of crime came to an end that night, but I learned a couple of lessons: not everyone is cut out for criminal work, and always carry a little cash in your socks, just in case Andy gets any more ideas.

FIZZIES: LUKEWARM NECTAR OF THE CHILDHOOD GODS

The other night I asked a bartender to do something I would probably never ask a plastic surgeon or auto mechanic to do- just *surprise* me. She came back with a drink she called a Nutty Monk- part coffee, part Frangelico and part Irish Cream. I said to myself this has got to be the most adult beverage I've ever tasted. The hazelnut flavor of the Frangelico mixed perfectly with the dark coffee, and the Irish Cream mellowed it all out. Absolutely delicious, I must say.

But if a Nutty Monk was the most *adult* beverage I'd ever tasted, then what would be my choice for the best *childhood* beverage? I had the usual suspects (chocolate milk, Nehi sodas, Chillee Willees and milkshakes), but I finally settled on the perfect drink of my earliest childhood- Fizzies.

Fizzies were produced by the fine people who brought us Alka-Seltzer, and after a few Nutty Monks I have begun to appreciate the irony. Fizzies came in the standard cola flavors, like orange, grape, lemon-line and a sort of coca-cola, but my favorite was the root beer. All a kid had to do was plop, plop and wait patiently for the fizz, fizz to die down. Few of us ever waited, which left us with that indescribable feeling of half a seltzer tablet sliding down our gullets. But oh, the flavors that would just burst out of the glass. A day without Fizzies was like a day without sunshine, so we would make sure that mom included them on her shopping list. I can still taste the last Fizzie I ever had.

Alas, Fizzies met an ignoble fate at the hands of modern science. The only sweeteners capable of withstanding the mysterious Fizzie manufacturing process were cyclamates, which were banned from use in American products around 1969. The last Fizzie plopped unceremoniously into its last glass of tap water around 1971 or so. I would like to think of that time as the day the bubbles died. I have found other beverages to replace Fizzies in my glass, but I haven't really found one to replace Fizzies in my heart. Maybe someday I'll ask a bartender to surprise me again, and he'll hand me a Rootbeer Fizzie on the rocks.

DEAD HOTDOG WALKING

If I were to slap a title on this essay, it would be 'Dead Hotdog Walking'. Many years ago, I attended a church which featured a youth service on Friday nights. We would play bible-centered versions of Charades or Twenty Questions, then perhaps have an object lesson on the wages of sin or the prospect of immediate Rapture. You know, the sort of topics that keeps impressionable twelve year old boys awake all night.

Following the service, we would all move to the Youth Center, which in our case was a refurbished tool and die shop. The adults would all grab a cup of coffee from the avocado green percolator and huddle around a communal table. The youth would play ping-pong, bumper pool or foosball. The more ambulatory amongst us would sneak off to the frozen custard stand and pig out on milkshakes. It was a good time to be alive and young in the frozen tundra of Northeastern Ohio.

But there was one part of the ritual that remains seared in my memory. The 70s were a time of great food experimentation-microwaves were common, hot air popcorn poppers were all the rage and I even remember a pre-George Foreman hamburger maker that did a great job with grilled peanut butter sandwiches. But the scariest thing of all was the hot dog cooker we used at the church. Talk about the most Vietnamesque way of cooking food. The cooker featured two sets of ominous looking spikes. The idea was to impale one end of a hot dog on a spike, then gently arch it over to the other spike. After the appropriate amount of convicts had been loaded onto Old Sparky, the warden would throw a switch and the hot dogs would be electrocuted to a turn. The lights would dim briefly, then we would pay our fifty cents and grab a dog or two. I believe cooler heads (or a few lawsuits) prevailed, and by the 80s we bid adieu to the scariest food preparation device in recent memory. I'm not sure, but I think there may be an object lesson on capital punishment in there somewhere. Who's up for a milkshake?

KEEF KNOWS WHAT TIME IT IS.

I believe we need to listen closer to our rock legends. Recently some linguists managed to compile a "Keith Richards to English, English to Keith Richards" dictionary and it turns out he was actually saying something important during interviews. Keith recently suggested that horses basically saved civilization as we know it. Consider all the important battles whose outcomes depended on the skills of men on horseback. Think about all the contributions draft horses made to improving labor. How far would we have gotten in the Old West if it hadn't been for Old Paint getting us there? I believe our beloved Rolling Stone and rehabilitation icon may be onto something here.

But what other discoveries or ideas can be credited with saving civilization from extinction? I got to thinking about that and came up with a few ideas of my own. First off, I think the creation of walls certainly changed things for the better. Dividing ourselves into smaller and smaller social units probably saved our collective sanity. Communal living might have protected early man, but walls provided a sense of 'self', which in turn promoted the formation of towns and cities. Of course you do have the problem of walls failing to live up to expectations- the Great Wall of China, Hadrian's Wall, the Berlin Wall, etc. Perhaps Frost was right when he wrote in his poem Mending Wall: 'Something there is that doesn't love a wall'. Some walls are good at uniting, while others are bent on division.

I also believe the cultivation of coffee has done a lot to define civilization. Coffee is a lingering reminder of the Ottoman Turk empire, which nearly conquered Europe 500 years ago. The exportation of a single coffee plant from France lead to the dominance of South American coffee growers in the world today. Coffee helped to equalize the economic playing field for many smaller countries struggling to find a viable commodity. Coffee was a staple item for settlers and pioneers, not to mention our fighting soldiers. Coffee became a nearly-universal beverage long before Coca-Cola and Pepsi. I'll even bet that coffee fueled more than a few late-night jams featuring Mick, Keith, Ronnie, Bill and Charlie. So it all comes full circle- horses, walls, coffee and

Keith Richards. I just know there's a future Jeopardy question in there somewhere.

COFFEE-METRICS

I notice that it's now the 21st century and our beloved country is still blatantly non-metric. Oh, we have the occasional two-liter soda bottle or the schizophrenic rulers marked with both inches and centimeters, but for the most part this is a metric-free zone. Look at it this way- entire countries in Europe have converted their money systems to Euros already, and we still have farthings, hectares and fathoms on our books. If nothing else, consider the fact we are about to be lapped by the Canadians on metric conversions. Doug and Bob McKenzie from the Great White North are closer to world unity than we are, eh?

What strikes me as particularly funny is how fast we Murkins converted to coffee-metrics.

Twenty years ago, coffee came in two sizes- small and large. For whatever reason, small was always TOO small and large approached Super Squishee proportions. Mugs, of course, were one size fits all- that is to say, bottomless. Then came the great gourmet coffee explosion of the late 80s and early 90s. The same Americans who had resisted speaking meters and liters into existence could suddenly order short, tall and grande coffees, without even once questioning the etymology. Heaven forbid I should pump three liters of gas into my tank, but give me a grande half-caf skinny soy mocha latte to go please.

I don't know if we'll ever go fully metric in this century, but I think it would be a great cosmic joke if all the gourmet coffeeshops agreed to change their ordering system to something out of the Wizard of Id comic strip. I would just like to hear one person order, in all seriousness, a 'frippin on the jimjam, frappin on the krotz'. I have this sinking feeling

I'll hear that long before I know how many kilometers it is to Disney World.

COFFEE NIPS: A GATEWAY CANDY?

I realized the other day that my first taste of coffee didn't come from a cup, but from a little piece of penny candy called a Coffee Nip. My dad used to take us to an indoor flea market on Saturdays, and one of the booths featured nothing but candy of every description. If we had a quarter or two, we could easily recreate the average Halloween haul. I fell hard for a piece of German-style chocolate called an Ice Cube. It wasn't like your average Chunky or Hershey Bar- it was incredibly smooth and creamy with a strong hazelnut flavor. At three cents a pop, it was the Cadillac of penny candies but I couldn't get enough of them. Our first and only goal on Saturdays was to seek out the 'Candy Lady' and load up our small brown paper bags.

On other days, we would ride our bikes up to a store called Reinker's, which was owned and operated by a sweet old German man. Mr. Reinker ran his store old-school style, with clerks that always knew your name and the best ice cream section in town. He would always insist on patting us on the head, which would simply offend our four year old sensibilities. As I grew older, I discovered that Mr. Reinker also stocked an incredible assortment of penny, nickel and dime candies. Just behind the cashier stood the Wall of Paradise, complete with Ice Cubes and Coffee Nips. But it didn't stop there, no sir. Reinker's carried the Holy Grail of collectibles for an eight year old kid- Wacky Packs. These were cards featuring spoofs of well-known products, like Dunder Bread and A-Jerks Cleanser. Each pack contained the ubiquitous stick of cardboard bubble gum, at least 5 stickers and a piece of a much larger puzzle. It was a glorious day when I actually had enough pieces to finish the mother of all things Wacky- the big puzzle.

I did some checking around the other day and found a supply of Ice Cubes online. They now go for thirty cents a piece. The Wacky Pack manufacturers cranked out their last run sometime in the late 80s or early 90s. The stickers I wasted as a child are now worth a fortune to serious collectors. I could be very sad about these twists of fate, but I'd much rather get another pat on the head from Mr. Reinker as he casually slips another Ice Cube into my mother's purse.

SO WHATEVER HAPPPENED TO SATURDAY MORNING CARTOONS?

This should teach me a little something about the pitfalls of nostalgia. I decided I would brew me up a nice pot of coffee, sit down in front of the tube and watch Saturday morning cartoons. EEEEEK! (ahem)

There was no Scooby Doo, no Bugs Bunny, no Laff-a-Lympics. Hell's bells, there wasn't even a Hong Kong Phooey. I found myself deeply mired in the muck and sludge that is Saturday morning cartoons today. I watched helplessly as anonymous bug-eyed heroines fought valiantly(?) against even more anonymous villains. Thankfully, I only had to endure about an hour of this onslaught until the networks decided I needed to watch sports or buy real estate at 10 am on a Saturday.

When I was a child, we were drawn to Saturday morning cartoons like hyperactive moths to a sugar-fed flame. We looked forward to seeing that genius Coyote set up his Rube Goldbergian house of cards in search of fresh Roadrunner meat. Apparently they just handed out genius cards to any old creature who wanted one, considering his abysmal success/failure rate. I actually remember keeping score during the Laff-a-Lympics, rooting for anyone who could wipe that smug grin off Snidely's face.

Now here's the plot to every cartoon on television: A band of cute Speed Racer look-alikes live in Harmonyville, USA. A heavily armored, gravel-voiced villain with anger management issues decides he wants to mess up their idyllic playground. The slowest of the good batch is either injured or captured by mindless henchmen. Only through teamwork and the aid of powerful laser technology can Cute triumph over lukewarm Evil, and said bad guy is promptly dispatched with extreme prejudice. Cute dolls sold separately, batteries not included.

I can understand that more mommies and daddies want to see news instead of Captain Kangaroo these days, but I sincerely hope cartoons make a glorious comeback in my lifetime. I've got serious money riding on the Coyote if they do.

THE MIRACLE THAT IS GOOD COFFEE

So here I am, sitting in my doctor's waiting room and thumbing through a magazine dedicated to high-end electronics and the platinum credit card holders who love them. Personally, I believe the doctors deliberately offer these selections so that we patients will understand what cool and exciting hobbies our diseases help finance.

I found an article on DVD players that absolutely changed my entire world view. Apparently these little black boxes are walking miracles of cutting-edge technology and we plebeians have the nerve to take them for granted. A typical DVD player has to make 3 billion calculations every second, and do it consistently for the entire run of the selected disk. One false move and it's time for our least favorite movie, Endless Loop. To put it in practical terms, trillions of precise calculations must be performed every time you want to enjoy a movie on DVD. Are you absolutely sure you want to see Ernest save Christmas?

That perfect cup of coffee you enjoy every morning is also a miracle, all things considered. Only the ripest beans can be selected for processing, which requires tremendous amounts of labor-intensive work. Coffee brokers must travel to warehouses in exotic and occasionally dangerous locations, bringing back only the beans that meet their employers' particular needs. Any professional coffee roaster will tell you how thin the margin can be between a successful roasting and unspeakable charcoal. If you grind your own beans, the subtle differences in sizes can easily turn your automatic drip masterpiece into a disastrous Warholian espresso.

Coffeemakers alone are a miracle of technology- water is held at just below boiling long enough for the filters to precisely control the flow through the grounds. If the water reaches boiling temperature, you could be left with coffee soup. Those paper filters have precisely enough permeability to allow coffee to flow through, but enough strength to hold back the unwanted solids. The result of all this precision is a delicious cup of gourmet coffee, any time you want one.

Sometimes the best miracles are right in front of us and we don't even know it.

CUPPING MIGHT JUST BE ONE OF THEM METAPHORS

The coffee world's equivalent of a professional wine tasting is called 'cupping', but don't expect to be invited to a local cupping and danish party any time soon. This is a practice best left to the professionals, if the preparation is any indication.

During a cupping session, individual coffees are ground and poured directly into small cups arranged around a large Lazy Susan affair. Hot (but not boiling) water is added, and the entire solution becomes a sort of coffee slurry. There's no fancy brewing or filtration involved- just coffee beans and water. The tasters spend much of their time absorbing the

fragrances of the selected coffees, then proceed to swirl and swish each cup's offerings with all the elan of their wine-tasting counterparts.

In general, the tasters are looking for strong flavors and a good mouthfeel. Copious notes are taken, since the economic future of a smaller plantation may hinge on the results.

But in the midst of all this research, I also discovered a life lesson or two. After the ground beans are mixed with water, a thin layer of residue often forms on the surface of the coffee. Tasters know that the coffee's most essential elements can be found underneath, so they will often place their noses directly over the coffee and 'break the crust'. It struck me how often we fail to do that in our own lives. We encounter new people every day, but we somehow forget to 'break the crust' in order to discover their truest qualities. Sometimes it seems our lives run on their own relentless turntables, but it helps to savor the richness of every cup we're presented.

I'll HAVE WHAT NILES CRANE IS HAVING

Coffee and television- now there's a combination just waiting to define a generation. 'Oh, these crazy kids, with their...coffee and their...television.' I'm beginning to feel like I've replaced sex, drugs and rock n roll with carbs, caffeine and NPR.

The other day I caught an episode of Seinfeld in which George accepts his date's invitation for late-night coffee, only to discover she actually MEANT it. He assumed 'going for coffee' was a euphemism for a more intimate encounter. "Who drinks coffee at midnight?" he bellowed to Jerry afterwards. I tend to agree with George more and more often these days, which is scary enough. Going out for coffee has become the invitation of choice for a lot of single people I know. It's really the perfect first date setup- intimate but public, non-threatening, non-intoxicating and conducive to making other plans for the evening — or not. It's an equally good setting for a quick getaway.

There is one thing I don't get about coffee shops on television, however. How is it that the most prominent piece of furniture in

Central Perk is always available to at least one Friend? Just try that trick at your own neighborhood coffee shop some time. Frasier's Cafe Nervosa is a little better about table-sharing, but I'd like to find a real waiter who knows what my 'usual' is. They say a goldfish's short term memory is so limited that every time he swims a lap, he discovers the castle all over again. I believe that gene has been passed on to an entire generation of coffee shop waiters. Of course, I do get a kick out of seeing Niles' reaction to even the slightest deviation from his usual order. 'You call this a 'whisper'of nutmeg? It's a full-throated SHOUT!'

I hope to find my own Central Perk or Cafe Nervosa someday, but until then I can still enjoy their presence on television. Now for the benediction- May your couch always be empty, and may the waiters all know your first name. Amen.

FULL SCALE YEMANA IN PROGRESS, REPEAT, *IN PROGRESS*

Did you know that in 16th century Turkey a man could be fined for not keeping his family coffeepot full? Only a scant 500 years later, a few of us should be arrested for doing just that. Few things disappoint more people in a shorter time than a pot of freshly-brewed bad coffee.

I got to thinking about the ancient Turkish solution to bad coffee, and I realized we actually have a patron saint of tarnished brew- Detective Nick Yemana from the TV sitcom "Barney Miller". Yemana's bad coffee was legendary among his co-workers, and when Jack Soo, the actor who played Yemana, passed away in 1979, the entire cast raised a mug in tribute. So I thought it might prove useful to provide 'Yemana Rights' to anyone accused of serving up less-than-ideal java:

'You have the right to grind your own beans.

Anything you do grind up will be filtered,

and served to you in a court of public opinion.

You have the right to clean water and clean equipment-if you cannot afford clean equipment, a Mr. Coffee will be issued to you

and charged to Joe DiMaggio's account.

You have the right to ask for a Starbuck's or SBC employee to be near you during questioning. If you cannot find a Starbuck's or SBC employee,

you're not trying hard enough.

Your coffee is presumed drinkable until proven otherwise in a court of law.

Unless, of course, the judge's clerk hands him the wrong mug. You may be toast.

You may have the right to reclaim any article of clothing used as a filter, but the court suggests you consider it an experiment that went horribly wrong.'

I can just see it now. "Coffee Squad", starring retired detective Nick Yemana and his band of cops-on-the-edge. They work 24 hours a day, 7 days a week, protecting the city from bad coffee makers everywhere.

'Boss, we just got a call from the Kinko's on 24th and Main. It sounds like a Code Sanka IN PROGRESS!' 'Bob, you and the new kid take this one. And be sure he gets Yemanaed real good. I don't wanna lose another one on a technicality!'

THE MATTRESS KING IS DEAD, LONG LIVE THE MATTRESS QUEEN

There's nothing like a good cup of gourmet coffee after the best night of sleep in your life.

I recently had a reason to put that theory to the test.

I've had the same mattress set for about 10 years now. To be even more accurate, I've endured sleeping on a Nerf pancake studded with dog-collar spikes for almost a decade. My wife and I decided it was time to look for a new mattress and box springs.

Long ago, I developed a hard and fast rule about furniture and bedding outlets. I swore I would never shop in any store that featured fictional characters- no Wizards, no Kings, no Elves, nothing of the sort. My *a priori* salesman was a guy named Chuck, of Honest Chuck's Mattresses and Beyond.

So here we are in the Hall of the Mattress King. Apparently the King was called away on royal business, so we were greeted by his son- the Mattress Duke, as it were. He invited us to try out any bed in the store, which translated to lying fully clothed on a bed while other customers watch the show. My wife and I became a pair of Goldilocks in a giant warehouse of Bear Family furnishings. We finally decided on a firm, but not TOO firm, mattress with a pillow top. In the store, it looked absolutely perfect.

A few days later, the bed of our dreams arrived by a most royal-looking delivery van. The men finished setting up the frame, boxspring and mattress, then had me sign for acceptance. After they left, I was left alone with my first new bed in years. And then I realized why it was so dark in the bedroom. This monolith was literally blocking out the sun. It was as if we rented a bed and they built an apartment around it to keep out the rain. We've now dubbed it Mount Bed-a-Rest. Oh sure, it's comfortable. We no longer count ceiling tiles to fall asleep- we ARE the ceiling tiles.

As far as the old mattress is concerned, I was really looking forward to a nice Viking funeral, courtesy of the King's coachmen. Instead, it ended up in a new neighbor's apartment 20 feet away. The night it finally showed up in a dumpster was the best night of sleep I ever had.

IN A GLASS THERMOS, NO ONE CAN HEAR SPOCK SCREAM

As I pour a fresh pot of coffee down my thermos, I'm reminded of all those thermoses (thermi?) which have come before.

I honestly couldn't say what the very first beverage I ever drank out of a thermos was, but my gut says Kool-Aid. I distinctly remember picking out an Aladdin Partridge Family lunchbox on that inevitable Back to School trek to our local K-Mart. I came ever so close to the outdated Star Trek model, but uncooler heads prevailed. Inside this seemingly indestructible casing was a matching thermos, complete with full-length drawings of Susan Dey, my future wife. I'd never seen a thermos up close before- it was still one of those Space Age deals. I eagerly screwed off the lid... the cup... the lid AND the cup. Darn, those astronauts are clever.

A brand new thermos has one of those distinctive smells, like a new car or grandma's bathroom. I looked at the shiny aluminized innards for a good long while. This thermos and I would share beautiful moments together- a steady companion in the uncertain world of second grade. As long as Lori Partridge was within my grasp, nothing could go wrong.

About twenty minutes later, something went horribly wrong. I grabbed a marble from the floor and casually dropped it down the gullet of my new thermos. In a moment worthy of the second choice Star Trek lunchbox crew, all heck broke loose. The sides of the thermos lining shattered, followed by a sudden explosion as the hull was breached and the vacuum of space claimed the remains. My Susan was a shattered collection of glass shards and broken dreams. The trip back to K-Mart was deafeningly silent. The store was completely sold out of Partridge Family thermoses, so I had to settle for what remained on the shelves.

Anyone know if a 1972 vintage Holly Hobby thermos is worth anything?

THE GREAT HYMNAL WAR

As I drink my coffee this morning, I think about my pseudo-career in music. I have always been interested in music, ever since I taught myself to play one of those wheezy Magnus chord organs when I was 4. The Magnus people made learning a breeze with their idiosyncratic numbering system. I still enjoy playing 5-6-5-3-5-6-5-3, and that beautiful love ballad 1-4-3-5-3-5. Eventually I took up the clarinet and learned a little something about music theory. Little did I know how much of an impact this early musical education would have on my life.

When I was 12, we joined the pew-jumping, chandelier-swinging church next door to our house. In reality it was an Apostolic Pentecostal church, but you know how rumors get started. The pastor was a firm believer in the encouragement of 'young people', which surely included me at the time. His wife was the church pianist, a young associate pastor was the organist, a family of country singers played guitars and yours truly became- the accordionist. My Magnus chord organ skills payed off in spades as I dutifully plowed through any song mentioning the Blood of the Lamb. One thing about Pentecostal music- the Blood had better be flowing, or else we're not playing it. For the four years I played in that orchestra, I was steeped in foot-stomping, hand-clapping good old gospel music.

Twenty some odd years later I find myself being asked to play the organ for a small country Methodist church in Alabama. Full of my former Pentecostal vim and vigor, I eagerly agreed to take on the challenge. Oh ye of little research. I found myself deeply embroiled in what can only be called the Great Hymnal War. The old hymnals could conceivably be divided into dirge/not dirge, while the absolute newest versions might as well have included 'Jesus is just alright with me'. Somewhere in the middle was the accepted hymnal, which incorporated just enough of both camps to be perfectly contentious to musicians. I'm actually enjoying the schizophrenia, as I quietly plug away on a real church organ every Sunday. But every once in a while, I find myself wanting to strap on an old accordion and see how strong those ceiling joists really are.

THERE'S MUSIC IN THAT THERE COFFEE, MISTER.

As I settle down to my final cup of coffee for the day, I hear the opening strains of Van Morrison's "Brown-Eyed-Girl" and realize how good life can get. I'm not sure what the most perfect song in the world would sound like, but I think John Prine is going to write it and Van Morrison is going to sing it. If they don't, I'm sure Tom Waits, Bruce Springsteen or Bob Dylan will be on ready five status.

Surprisingly enough, coffee shows up in a lot of memorable songs. Mickey Dolenz promises time for "coffee-flavored kisses and a bit of conversation" in the Monkee's *Last Train to Clarksville.* Don Williams begins his lonesome day with "coffee black, cigarette" in his country hit *Some Broken Hearts Never Mend.* Bob Dylan lingers over *One More Cup of Coffee* before facing (*The Valley Below*). Oddly enough, I don't believe the Beatles ever mentioned coffee in their music, but one might wonder what was in the cup Paul speaks of in *A Day in the Life.* Coffee is almost always the one bit of normalcy that creeps into the songwriter's otherwise complicated verses. We can all identify with that desperate search for the waitress, or that early morning jolt of reality only coffee can bring.

For a long time, I thought Van Morrison's *Into the Mystic* was as close to perfection as anyone could get. Now I'm beginning to think that we are all responsible for writing our own perfect song, one where the verses don't really matter and all our friends know the chorus by heart.

YOU KNOW THAT WE ARE LIVING IN A COFFEE WORLD

My wife tells me that she's been drinking coffee since she was four years old, and somehow I believe her. It may be the dozen or so cans of Story House gourmet coffee strewn around the house, or it may be the fact that we are already on our third coffeemaker in six years of marriage. We can't leave the local coffeeshop/bookstore without gazing longingly at the top-end cappucino machines and French press carafes on the shelves. You know those oversized bins of whole bean coffee at the grocery store? I'm beginning to think they're actually free gumball machines for coffee fanatics.

My wife says she started her coffee habit by finishing off the dregs of coffee left behind by her parents. My brother started drinking coffee at our mother's funeral. He started off with equal proportions of cream, sugar and coffee, then eventually acquired a taste for the stronger stuff. Being an inveterate hot tea drinker from way back, I still prefer a little cream and sugar in mine. My first real exposure to coffee was not in a cup, but one of those chewy coffee-flavored candies. I took one bite, expecting chocolate, and received a rather abrupt introduction to the world of coffee.

Some say the world is divided into two groups- those who like Neil Diamond and those who don't. I say that the world can be divided in a different way- the world we knew before coffee, and the one we discovered after that first cup. 'Coffee World' is inherently different- life has a few more edges, a little more color. Like any other first experience, you can sense that an invisible border has been irreversibly crossed, but somehow you don't seem to mind the change. Coffee World can be a challenging place sometimes, but its also worth trying all the way to the dregs.

WHAT'S NEXT—COFFEE-FLAVORED COFFEE?

I've been on a diet for about 6 months now, which explains why I just finished eating a bowl of coffee almond ice cream. Let he who is without carb cravings cast the first Slimfast can. Speaking of diet drinks, I believe more than a few companies have composed coffee-flavored variations on their standard liquid fare. Oh they try to be so clever by calling it 'mocha', but we see through their little ruse.

Over the years, there have been many attempts to blend coffee with another food or beverage. Some have proven hugely successful, while others have fallen a little short of the glory. Coffee ice cream came straight out of the vat with a halo and a large bow saying 'Buy me, I'm terrific!', while the earliest versions of cold cappucinos played cards on the shelves and said 'When you run out of every other drink in the house, you know where I live.' Times have changed, and now frozen or chilled cappucinos are among the most popular drinks in gourmet coffeehouses. Sometimes it just comes down to building the perfect beast and waiting for the right consumers to find it.

As appealing as it sounds, there is one coffee-enhanced beverage I'm glad hasn't made it onto store shelves-Drew Carey's infamous Buzz Beer. For those of you who missed the show, Buzz Beer came about after one of Drew's cronies started drinking coffee between taste tests. The combination proved to be marketable on the show, but I seriously doubt anyone would actually try to duplicate it in real life. Coffee has been used in a lot of strange concoctions, but beer seems to do best on its own. (At least I won't be polishing off a pint of beer pistachio ice cream any time soon). That's okay, though- it leaves more room in the fridge for my card-playing iced cappucino buddies.

THERE'S A DAY FOR THAT

I happen to be the proud owner of the most oxymoronic job title in the world- a professional poet. Historically, this has proven to mean I'll be long gone before the check for the pizza arrives. We poets live for April, which happens to be National Poetry Month. For a solid thirty days, poetry and poets can roam freely in the streets, without calling their parole officers or violating restraining orders.

April also happens to be National Coffee Month, which makes some sort of symbiotic sense to me. Coffeehouses were generally the first venues to embrace poets, so I can see sharing a month with the hands that feed us. All this talk about national months got me to thinking, though. You have to figure that for every month that makes sense (Black History Month, AIDS Awareness Month, Women in Sports Month, etc.) there must be hundreds that are best described as answers to obscure trivia questions. Creating a new 'Month' must be the bread-and-butter of legislators everywhere. It's got to be the best win/win situation of all time- instant respect for the lawmakers, and recognition of the oft-ignored blue-backed iguana owners of America.

I'd like to know who decides what cause deserves a national Day, Week, Month or Year. The negotiations have got to be the most delicate diplomatic operations in Washington DC: 'You know, Bill, I share your love for the little critters myself, but how about National Wombat DAY? We had to give Senator Jones "National Pantyhose Month", so the calendar's looking a little full right now.' No matter what the occasion, I'd like to think someone is waiting for the Wombat Parade of Heroes to pass by on that special day.

All I know is that next April, I will be sipping my gourmet coffee and working on my next collection of poems. If you care to join me, just remember I like extra pepperoni.

RITUAL—THE OLDEST WORD IN ANY LANGUAGE

As I sip my first cup of coffee this morning, I'm struck by how much of our lives are defined by ritual. Our morning routines are actually rituals in casual clothing, and without them our day is a goner already.

When I was a child, Sunday morning was the best ritual of all. Mom would start frying bacon on our gas stove around 9 o'clock or so. By the time I rolled out of bed, it would reach the gurgling and splattering stage. The sun would be streaming through our dining room window, and the air felt different than other days. As the bacon continued to fry, my mother would start boiling hot tea in a dented aluminum pot set aside for such a purpose. There was rarely any sense of urgency on Sunday morning- things were going to happen organically, and we understood that.

The bacon would eventually become these burnt stalks of unidentifiable pork, but I looked forward to each and every piece. Mom would scramble some eggs and fry them in the remaining bacon grease. Our breakfasts consisted of cholesterol, sodium and caffeine, but I wouldn't have traded them for the world. It was a ritual that held us together until it was time for church. To this day, I still ask for burnt bacon wherever I go.

So this morning I drank my coffee, watched a little news and made my way to my new church, in my new life as a grown-up. I realize now that we are all responsible for our own rituals, even if they no longer involve cartoons, dented aluminum tea pots or those who made them possible.

NEW WORDS FOR THE COFFEEHOUSE GENERATION

I'm always on the search for words that should exist but don't. The other day I tried out two new ones, *wifittude* and *husbanality*. *Wifittude* is what husbands receive when their *chore* list becomes an *ignore* list. *Husbanality* is a generic term for all those stories your spouse insists on retelling, under the mistaken belief that they are universally hilarious.

Here are some new words for the coffee house generation:

Slurgle: The first tentative sip of coffee you take before deciding if it's safe to swallow.

Janglicide: Unilateral decision that the only way to cure your caffeine shake is with *more coffee*.

Shotophobia: Irrational fear that your shot of hazelnut syrup will turn out to be bubblegum-flavored instead.

Grande Envy: Noticing the KFC-chicken-bucket-sized-cups everyone else seems to be ordering.

Javachum: Those irresistible candies and snacks which only seem to taste right with gourmet coffee.

Brevado Delirium: Ordering your coffee in the grand style of Niles Crane, only to end up with a cup of hot water and an oreo cookie.

Mochavision: The perceived ability to see through walls after five shots of espresso.

Brewfluvia: The pile of empty sugar packets, candy wrappers, coffee cups and napkins left by the previous occupants of your prized corner table.

Browzilla: Bookstore code for a patron who skims through every best-seller while nursing a 50 cent cup of coffee.

"Jaux Pas": Any mistake made while ordering which results in suppressed laughter from the staff.

SELECTIONS FROM "Makebelieve Ballroom" and "Collateral Damage Report"

Abandoning Red Hill

'Now it is a vineyard, like so many others;/But when you taste its wine, you drink the blood of your brothers.' From Red Hill, a French folk song.

I let someone else do the driving for a little while-
I watched the lines blur behind us, each racing after the next,
towards some vanishing point just beyond the Stuckey's sign;
I am abandoning Red Hill again.
I screamed to get in there many years ago,
trapped between Heaven and a birthing table,
taking in just so much air to mark some territory.
No, my feet don't fit my legs too well,
if lamp-burnt movies don't lie.
I spent more time falling in those badly-lit days;
I was learning to stand like a man, like a Midwest farmer man-
until push came to shove, and I retired my number.
I am abandoning Red Hill again, and the weight of it scares me-
I will no longer have forts to defend from night-time attack,
and defenseless clay soldiers will have to fend for themselves.
(I will be back for you, I promise.)
Now the asphalt-hard truth is staring holes right through me-
Red Hill will never leave me, will never turn me away;
Red Hill will always be mine for the asking;
(I could never ask for more from any other memory.)
Pull over, I'm ready to drive now.

ATTICUS RESTS

We should all sweat long
    enough to meet the man
    who beat the law of averages.
    This man is not the sum of his words,
    but the total of his actions.
    The books grow colder, the papers scatter,
    the disciples pray elsewhere;
    but the teacher (oh! the teacher)
    is still with us.
    The house seems smaller, the children older,
    the grass grows higher;
    but the father (oh! the father)
    is still with us.
    We seek your country simple answers, Atticus.
    Oh, to hear that same old story yet again,
    (you know the one)
    about that car, that man, that job,
    that summer in the Army,
    that diner at the edge of town,
    that angel who changes tires,
    that homecoming game, that dance,
    that girl from Jasper...
    Tell me that story again, and this
    time I swear I'll listen.
    We who remain will continue to rise
    from the balcony at your passing-
    We who remember will continue to bless
    whatever food we are given-
    We who live on will continue to follow
    the examples you left for us-

We who knew you will continue
to try to know ourselves.
We should all sweat long
enough to meet the man
who beat the law of averages.
Now Atticus may rest.

Auxiliaries

The five older ladies have poured their tea again,
    And look to each other for recognition.
    This has been quite a summer, yes it has,
    And Charles and William and my boy Walter
    Have really taken a shine to their new garden,
    Says one, steadying her cup for emphasis.
    The others agree on summer, it is noted.
    The gladiolas should start to bloom any day now,
    My daughter Caroline so loves the flowers behind the house
    Now that she has more time to visit,
    Says another, cleaning her glasses for attention.
    Most agree on the blooming time for gladiolas, for the record.
    I tell you what, if the city doesn't start doing something
    About the noise, I just don't know what I'll do,
    Some days I just can't read my books like I want to.
    Says a third, sipping her tea for good measure.
    The noise situation is acknowledged, and receives sympathy.
    The five older ladies have finished their tea collectively,
    And Edith, bless her heart, can't find her medication.
    The others agree fully that they ought to make it easier.
    And I wonder sometimes if Walter's garden and the gladiolas
    and the noisemakers and the pharmacists shouldn't just get
    together like this, and discuss a few things over tea and cake,
    Says a writer, wiping his eyes dramatically for effect.
    But no one votes on this issue,
    And the meeting sinks back into the
    primordial woodwork.
    (It's at my house next week, if you're interested.)

Brady's Leap

I sit beside the Cuyahoga creek
    and wonder how he done it-
    Pursued by motivated Native Americans
    across the burning Midwestern grass,
    until he found himself caught
    between the Devil and the wide blue stream.
    Captain Brady never hesitated,
    never reconsidered,
    never admitted defeat for one minute.
    In that great key to the city moment,
    Captain Brady (and horse)
    flew majestically
    over the raging creek to safety.
    We have a coffee shop named in his honor now.
    Don't laugh.
    A lot of brave people have decided to leap
    after a little too much cappucino.
    You know how in life things just happen,
    and you search the skies for answers,
    and you throw the I Ching for giggles,
    and you consult the charts for direction?
    Well, on those days when indecision
    has got the best of you,
    I want you to consider the Captain Brady
    approach with an open mind.
    I just got on my horse one day and leapt-
    and just kept on leaping.
    I leapt right out of Kent,
    right out of Ohio,
    right out of America,

right out of this planet,
right out of this galaxy,
right on out to the farthest reaches.
It was then I realized that the Indians weren't chasing me.
I realize now that this constitutes some sort
of personal breakthrough,
and believe me I appreciate that and all,
but the real question for me now is-
Does this sort of thing
warrant my own coffee shop?

Breath of a Child's Undoing

Spring and breeze and such were oh so powerful then-
    I fiddled and I fiddled and I fiddled
    while Rome was still smoking;
    I danced and I whittled
    and I climbed and I giggled,
    and drank the finest of barrelled rainwater.
    I was no match for Earth, metaphorically speaking-
    She found me once at the end of a ramp,
    She reached for me at the height of my swinging career,
    She confounded me with her dandelions.
    I should not ask for better teachers
    than Sun and breeze and such-
    for in their memorials are found
    the blocks of who we were;
    for in their branches are found
    the lilacs of our renovations,
    for in their arms is cradled
    the breath of a child's undoing.
    (People should ask what I am doing here,
    all alone and uninvited.
    I should have asked what I had done here,
    so small and unrequited.)

Bringing the Wendy's

Just clang on the lamp if you need anything, mom.
I'll just be lying here, thinking about how small morphine is,
And how large life is going to get in six months to a year.
No, you are not wasting away on me yet.
You still have report cards to sign, and P.T.A. brownies to build;
You still have to ask me how goggles work,
You still have to touch my blue ribbons for third grade poetry.
You have obligations, my beautiful, half-dying mother.
Obligations.
But right now all I want is to see you breathe better
and stay regular.
It's the little urinary victories that matter most today.
Your legs bend so well today,
You should be kidding yourself about walking any day now.
My delusional mother is dreaming
about walking to Reinker's again.
I love my delusional mother today.
Once, I walked on good son legs all the way up to Wendy's.
I brought you a chicken sandwich, with bacon just to tease you.
That bite you took sustained you for a day or so.
You told all the relatives that your son brought you a Wendy's.
It's been fifteen years now, and I haven't ordered one since.
(If you need anything, world, just clang on the lamp.
I'll just be lying here, thinking about how small life can get.)

Brother Judd

The fish could hardly be expected to remember us-
    Two sleep-dusted Ohio boys, working a pole with Brother Blake,
    methodically plinking the glass of Heritage Lake.
    He was a most agreeable fisherman, long since passed on,
    but he understood the principle of the thing itself;
    this sport of tricking one live into becoming a trophy or dinner
    for those other lives with nothing better to do.
    I loved Brother Blake, I really did.
    He of the Pentecostal faith (one God one Name one Baptism)
    who spoke kindly to my mother, as he rushed her sons
    to rattle the baitman's door;
    We need us some frantic cold red worms;
    We need us some possessed nightcrawlers;
    Do we got any of them salmon eggs anywhere?
    Fish don't bite on 'em anyway.
    (They know their own.)
    Once, I caught a beauty-
    a rainbow trout, with all the hidden
    colors of the Lord, he said,
    and my friend, who had no grasp
    on the subtleties of angling,
    bent the fish clean in two,
    just to show it could be done.
    Brother Blake, his patience at an end,
    said, "Son, don't be foolish with those fish."
    So we put it back in the creel,
    feeling much like the fish must have felt
    when he felt that first tug.
    I don't fish much now at all.
    but occasionally I catch myself thinking

about that elder of my childhood church,
and start feeling a little foolish
about all the beautiful Fish
I've bent in two since then.

Cleft for Me

Four small whispers can now leave rehearsal,
    the last cigarette has been ground to ashes.
    It was once important for us to kill some Negroes,
    no matter how many times they claimed to fear God—
    no matter how pretty their dime store dresses were—
    no matter how late they were for choir practice.
    In the whole of Birmingham, 1963,
    freedom smelled a lot like gunpowder residue
    on the hands of Bobby Frank Cherry.
    Four shadows from another mangled storm shelter
    can now share Cokes on hot summer revivals
    and find Sister Henrietta's eyeglasses for her.
    While I draw this
    fleeting breath,
    When my eyes
    shall close in
    death,
    I shall fly
    to worlds unknown,
    And behold thee
    on thy throne.
    Now is the day four little singers
    found their way back
    to the 16th Street Baptist church,
    after getting lost in another man's smoke.

COLLATERAL DAMAGE REPORT

'If it is in your power to decide,
   why do you do it? But if in another's,
   whom do you find fault with-
   the atoms or the gods?
   Either is madness.' Marcus Aurelius, Meditations

Let us skip, you and I,
   through certain half-smelted streets;
   where time and conscience dissolve like watches,
   and glass shadows catch the first sun's rays
   fully on their mistaken faces.
   (In the tents the orphaned come and go,
   Cursing poor Michaelangelo.)
   I am becoming more flesh than bone here,
   No longer thirsty for what the architects have dropped,
   No longer hungry for scraps of Oppie's wet dreams.
   No longer driven to swallow the Rebel flag whole.
   I could use a quick dousing
   of napalm here in my soul,
   there are fires I could never put out;
   I could use a spill of cluster
   bombs to clear my head,
   I have stains that will never wash out.
   (In the quonset, survivors
   come and go, jealous
   of Michaelangelo.)
   There was talk today between
   my god and your god,

and my god rained down fire
upon working-class Sodom-
and my god rained down vengeance
on industrial Gomorrah-
and my god spoke with furious anger,
and terrible wisdom-
So your little tin god spoke to his people
in his little tin voice,
and surrendered everything
he had ever wanted.
(In the new world,
poets will come and go,
still reeling
from Michaelangelo.)

Crusader Rabbit

I picked up my first stray when I was five, and it promptly died.
    He was a fine catch, as strays go -
    Strong in spirit, eminently playful, relatively grateful;
    But he soon discovered the highway the hard way,
    And I discovered that traffic does not slow down for grieving boys.
    As my growing was given out to me, my strays took on other shapes.
    Impractical birds with one good wing, indecipherable bluegill and
bass;
    Indecisive chickens and the occasional Easter bunny -
    To each, I gave my pre-adolescent heart and cartoon soul,
    Until they had reached their respective Heavens.
    And now I find my strays are called people.
    These are the ones who don't respond to makeshift bandages,
    Or necessarily appreciate the off-key comfort songs
    Of cradling crusader rabbits with haloes to match.
    Let them go, let them go, you must let them go -
    They are strays, and will carry you off to their own funerals-
    They are strays, and will find other chocolate-covered hands to feed
them -
    Let them go, let them go, you must let them go -
    They are strays, and filled with the rage of previous owners -
    They are strays, and drunk with the knowledge of other highways.
    What I have done, I have done for Love.
    And what I failed to do, (oh, what I failed to do)
    Why I did that for Love as well.
    Love sure takes a beating from crusader hypocrites like me.

CUIDADO

all pardons on us, most heavenly father,
    for we have had your wives for breakfast.
    revolution should be a poor man's fist,
    covered in shit and fleeting promises;
    we do not deal in subtleties here,
    this is not a finishing school.
    georgia's beautiful in the summertime,
    when young men's fancies turn to rape;
    georgia's lovely in the wintertime,
    when old despots' thoughts turn to action.
    when the peepholes start squealing freedom, freedom-
    who am i to stand on their filthy necks,
    who am i to display their broken bodies,
    who am i to enjoy the fruits of their children?
    i am the well-trained way, der Truth, das Light,
    no man comes to know power but through me,
    i am the grass that grew high at Austerlitz,
    (i still work.)
    pardons on all of us,
    ye heavenly hosts,
    for we have used your servants
    as bulletin boards.

Jerusalem Engines

The city walls pulse with the knowledge of soldiers' fears,
I have no hint of weaponry: nay, not one;
The torchlights swagger with the threat of daughters' tears,
I have no sense of history: nay, not one.
She appears to me with the promise of sweeter days to come,
I have no time for leniency: nay, not now;
She comforts me with the dulcimer, the psaltery, the drum;
I have no room for sympathy: nay, not now.
Death is now my brother, and my brother calls me out by name,
I no longer have a soul to speak of: nay, not one;
Men will lay in linen by my hand, their eyes will speak my shame,
I no longer have a land to return for: nay, not one.
She returns to me with the solace of unbroken dreams to be,
I have no fear of redemption: nay, not now;
She anoints me with her oils, she soothes me with her mystery,
I have no cause to lose her love: nay, not now.
We built engines in Jerusalem
To darken our fallen land,
In my house, it shall be said,
Love dared to show its hand.

LIVING IN PETRA

So is this your first
    time in Baltimore,
    this woman asks,
    and I tell her no,
    I'd been here before,
    in another life,
    as a soft-shelled crab.
    As I recall,
    it ended badly
    for me then, too.
    So is this your first
    time in Cleveland,
    the bus driver asks,
    and I say no,
    I'd been here before,
    in another life,
    as a frontiersman.
    As I recall,
    I ended up in
    a ditch back then, too.
    So is this your first
    time out of the country,
    this attendant asks,
    and I tell her no,
    I'd been overseas before,
    in another life,
    as a fighter pilot.
    Seems like I caught
    a lot of flak
    back then as well.

So is this your first
time in Petra,
this Bedouin asks,
and I say yes this time.
All things considered,
I believe living in
a pile of rocks
would be most prudent.

Love and Lagniappe

This is how easily two stiff souls
    can learn to bend,
    And pivot around the mulberry times
    Like dancers,
    defining their time and space.
    I find my portion has mingled with your portion,
    Losing nothing in the exchange,
    And leaving all doubt in its wake.
    This is how perfectly two wounded birds
    can learn to sing,
    And sweep away the ghosts of the hunters
    With authority, not wanting for anything.
    I find my journey has intersected
    with your journey,
    Losing no ground in the meeting,
    And abandoning all fear in the flight.
    You are in word and in spirit my certain Ballerina,
    And I celebrate our dance every day.

Makebelieve Ballroom

and when all that remains of
      our dimestore dances are scuffs
      on aching linoleum,
      I shall consider you carefully,
      and know that we were gods once.
      this was how the rockefellers
      played it, all hot and close
      enough to the bones;
      we blew eight to the bar,
      eight to the bar,
      on blistered rugs and buckling
      storeroom floors.
      and you were all fierce reds
      and polished whites,
      clapping and surging with
      the pulses of Dorsey,
      whirling and crackling with
      the promises of Miller,
      turning and wailing with
      the heat of the vacuums.
      Today, I played the Dorsey
      once more,
      and as the needle danced
      back and forth
      on only a paper moon
      only a paper moon
      only a paper moon,
      I heard the creaking
      of the storeroom
      boards, and for one

dying moment
you and I were spooning,
alone and invincible,
in the dust of
our makebelieve ballroom.

Modern Cuts for Modern Men

His father ran the power company like a cheap Swiss watch,
    as the last of the cuts poured out blood and Mad Dog,
    mama's precious blue-eyed drunk lay gutted and silenced,
    gutted and silenced on Huntsville city property.
    Olan Mills had no idea what they once captured on film,
    Tom and Vivian and their two small ideas for boys;
    each looking so bright and sober that morning,
    the combs finding no reluctance, no resistance, no defiance.
    One would grow to be every father's waking dream,
    a Marine so pulled and taut and inspection-ready,
    drawing his service revolver so smoothly from its home
    one might never feel the sting.
    The other would not show up in any more wallet-sized pictures,
    nor would he ever agree to pass the plate in church again,
    This other son would fail to keep his promises to God and country,
    finding himself mired in piss and Jack and shattered glass bottles.
    His father would identify the body in his own sweet time,
    but the police said a homeless man was already in custody;
    A jogger found the body sprawled over some battered suitcases,
    his one acceptable arm already pointed towards home.

Oven

I see in her mottled skin
    such visions
    of dishwater pain,
    The desperately overturned
    second-hand furniture,
    stripped bare of our lunch money.
    Here in the crispest of mornings
    lies purpose- in oatmeal, in Praise the Lord,
    in sitting still while the tea boils;
    Here in the emptiness of my third grade,
    she is free to be trapped in polyester,
    free to consider all the worlds
    her hands have had to make from scratch.
    (He is a forgetful bastard this morning,
    all caught up in his steering gears
    without a drop of change.)
    So this is what warmth can be,
    as we huddle by the gas oven for heat,
    and stare holes through the blue flames.
    She is not my mother this morning-
    She is a scalloped-skinned mutt,
    carefully trampling down the circles
    where she may find tea-stained redemption.
    I would tell you more,
    but sometimes yellow
    trucks stop by,
    to rescue small children
    from all matters human.

Pinaud's Tonic

Five disabled dollars later, this man is cleansed-
    Briefly allowed to borrow some human sunlight
    On another stranger's bench.
    His heart is now as hard as a claymore,
    Pointed at some forgotten enemy,
    Beating eight to the bar
    like some slopehead jukebox,
    Pulsing with the bagged donations
    of o-positive neighbors back home.
    The barber sweeps away the remnants
    of this man's raincatchers;
    He knows how close they were
    to being brothers to the dragon-
    He has breathed its jellied fire before;
    He shut that door with a shiny trade school license,
    His talk gets smaller as the years allow.
    For six hungry weeks, this man could be Westmoreland himself,
    Safe in the knowledge that anyone could love him;
    He could limp and clang
    with the best of fatted Rotarians,
    Eating the center of the rubber chicken
    every Monday at twelve.
    His neck stiffens in the breeze
    with the steady burn of Pinaud's Tonic,
    He has become temporary master of all he can remember,
    He rises to greet his brethren with a one-legged kiss,
    He embraces the illusions of a town that evaded him.
    (I gave him a cup of water, and he spilled it all over the place.)

URIM AND THUMMIN

Your tattooed stigmata is showing, my dear-
    that spot of willful blood lies dormant;
    while greedy hosts of Angels draw illicit lots,
    and seek redemption in performance.
    I may cast off now into more uncertain seas,
    now that the winds have finished their shift;
    I sing the shanty songs of unbroken sailors,
    now that my heart is allowed to drift.
    You have no hold on me, my tortured mercury dancer,
    now that our final sails have failed us;
    for if Fate were a captain, and we were the sea-
    the poor Bloke should never have sailed us.

Washing Day

she never once minded the dust,
as he carried them both into
town, his mind filled with thoughts
of discounted hardware.
she may have even wished him
the worst, as his levi's tumbled
and crashed in endless waves,
losing their color by degrees,
as the years broke down like oil.
she spooned off lumps of Sarah's homemade
alone and crossthreaded on a folding table,
as he tossed baling wire and made due
with yesterday's donut and machined coffee.
As soon as Nathan's growed,
she shuddered as she folded, but
there was so much left to unspoken
chance, as the road back stayed
just as dry as they had left it.
it would be years before
she learned the same screen
door that opens wide on
the one side can stay so
desperately shut on the other.

CAMBODIAN MUSIC

Pol Pot's deflowered now
who used to ride a water-
smooth buffalo
and kill onetwothreefourfive
million traitors
Justlikethat—Jeezus,

he was an awful liar,
and what I'd like to know is
how do you like your despot now,
mister Death?

The Cambodians are divided
    into two camps now:
    Those under the age of 25,
    and those who never thought
    they would ever be 25.
    This plays hell on radio
    demographics and advertising
    targeting, but the ones
    who ate the most lizards
    generally don't have
    much buying power.
    Old Pol Pot knew this-
    He knew that intellect killed revolutionaries-
    so he murdered all the teachers.
    Old Pol Pot knew all this—
    He knew that children
    were the way of thefuture,
    so he had them dismembered
    in front of their mothers-
    (Don't worry- witnesses say the
    children were bashed against
    the walls first, to soften them up)
    Old Pol Pot knew all about these things-
    He studied them at school in Paris.
    He knew that city folks don't take well to strangers.
    so he had them all herded out to the fields-

The lucky ones died on the first day.
Old Pol Pot knew a lot of things, he did.
He knew that men with eyeglasses
might become intellectual,
so he had them all shot in the street.
Old Pol Pot did much
for child labor, he did.
He put the revolutionary
children to work every day,
whacking in the skulls
of tired elderly women,
sometimes taking bets
on how many swings it would take.
Old Pol Pot understood the needs
of modern corporations, he did.
He single-handedly downsized
a country of 5 million redundant farmers
into a more manageable
3 million terrified refugees.
(He believed strongly in agrarian reform,
long before it became fashionable.)
Cambodians love their music now.
Cambodians love to hug their surviving
children, and tell them stories
about lands filled with fish and bread.
Thanks to a frail old man
named Pol Pot,
(who holed up for years
in the jungles of his own making)
Family reunions are now optional in Cambodia.

KILL THE KING, LEO

It is night again,
and my grandmother June
and my great-hunchbacked
Uncle Leo are playing poker again.
The water is undrinkable here,
unless you douse it with Kool-aid,
or better yet- forget the water and go
straight to whiskey,
as my grandmother June
and my great- hunchbacked
Uncle Leo are doing
as they play poker again.
We are so small tonight, my brother and me,
hunkered down low in our cousin's bed
to avoid my grandmother June
and my great- hunchbacked
Uncle Leo as they slowly die,
(Drunk and alone),
playing poker downstairs again.
'This is the King, Leo!
You know what you must do
to the King, don't you?
This is the King.
You've got to kill it, Leo...'
'Oou dunk, joon.
I not gau ta kill the king.
Oou dunk, joon.'
'Leo, gawd damn you-
It's the damn King,
and if you don't kill the son-of-a-bitch,
I will, gawd damn you.'

'Oou tarred, joon.
Oou go bed now
I wan to see the moo tows.'
(moo cows)
So the King did not die that night,
nor any other night my Grandmother June
and my great-hunchbacked
Uncle Leo played poker and drank whiskey,
dead and alone in the kitchen.
I learned years later
that my grandmother June's
first and only king had fallen
on Anzio Beach in 1944,
making Western Pennsylvania
safe for unemployed coal miners
and alcohol salesmen.
So one night, I went downstairs
and played penny poker with Grandma June,
and my late hunchbacked Uncle Leo,
and this time the King was spared
by a grandson who finally
learned the score.

COURTESY DANCE

(Wee swing) we swing, we dip, we dive-
With a whoop(sorry!)whoop(sorry!)whoopwhoopwhoop-
With a swing(batterbatter), swing(batterbatter)swingswingswing-
And we thump!(how we thump) And we thump!(how we thump),
'Til we bump:(cha cha cha), 'Til we bump:(cha cha cha)
Just give a little hand to the gent next door,
Hope that the band can play some more,
Find all the glitter on that old wood floor,
Find all the glitter on that old wood floor.

You get down the fiddle and you rosin up your life,
Pull up the flowers and give them to the wife;
You dance like the devil's coming over for dinner,
And you're serving him crow, 'cause you ain't no sinner,
And you're serving him crow, 'cause you ain't no sinner.

HAIKU

Darkness, and what stays
Falls too close to the heart-Poor
enough for beggars.
My tears have failed me-
Brushed off like so much laughter,
My breath leaps before.
Gandy dancers sing,
the iron is forced to obey
their undying song.
Entering wisdom
Is the first sign of passion,
And love's last gamble.

MONEY, MARBLES OR CHALK

I broke our deal, ol' meestah meestah-
I put two and two together,
(and all I gots for my
troubles was the troof.)
Whattum I sposed to do wit dat, anyways?
You and me, we coming to blows real soon, meestah-
You can grin all you wants to;
You can laugh yerself to death if you feel lak it,
(You ain't werf scrapin off my shoes.)
I takes to eatin' your dirt in spells,
you nasty old goat-
You thinks yer so cool to fill
a man's belly up with lies,

Yer thinking days is coming to a close, brother,
if I has ta wipe the blade off myself.
What you does to me ain't gonna matter no more,
But you does it to my family all damn day,
And I's tired of you eatin' up my spirit, meestah meestah.
I'm movin' what's mines
to places you ain't nevah been,
And we gonna be fine,
And we gonna shine,
And we gonna drink wine,
And we gonna be fine,
And we gonna shine,
And we gonna drink wine.
(And I's gonna live like a man
whose werf ain't connected
to the price of cardboard.)

ORION'S WOUND (FOR KURT COBAIN, THE EMISSARY)

We let ourselves become so damned comfortable,
here in our crowded rocks-
and you let yourself become so damned vulnerable,
there on your battered island-
What I knew of life,
you selfless bastard,
I had begun to accept.
What you learned from life,
you helpless shepherd,
you had begun to disown.
Explain your answer in words I understand,
Mister Cobain.
Suck the naked mystery out of this
fucking lie of yours;

You felt the fire in your belly,
until you could feel no more-
Now feel our fires,
you tortured puppet.
I'm pissed off, Kurt, so I do the little word dance
on your brave little head;
I'm confused, Kurt, so I do the the little
morbid shuffle for the unwashed dead.
You're a little hippie hero to the
sheep who want your songs.
DEAD HEROES SUCK.
No apologies.

TERRIBLE TRUTH CONCERNING MOTES AND BEAMS

I will see in her terribled)face all flesh:all one,
Spitting by degrees
down UNBLEST
sturm greats(
She,
who
(fellow me,
fellow
me close
now)
shrieks!her royal stinkrot petty coot
at allwhatwouldhearher not-
'a plague fer alla youse;
(hopes ye all choke
on.yer.bluddy.money.
ye.godless.heathuns.)
And I turn it square back on you:
You who would rather sh*t,& call it p ro gre sss)

I will not dance your likker dance,
(and hike the skirts of all mankind)
As long as there are desert underpasses
where Children still
feed air
to the other
pigeons.

BLUE 88

felt the warm and sudden spray
of the sergeant's French Silk Stockings,
as he lay half-sprawled on the beautiful,
oh so beautiful, oh so beautiful,
freshly-fallen snow.
opened up, yes lord, really opened up
my store-bought British cigars
and gave the Krauts holy bloody hell,
while little grateful girly girlies
danced on our open bellies.
oh! the nights we had together,
my sweet sweet Marie,
nestled in the entrails
of some guy who smoked luckies,
(and could not run to save
his life magazines)
I felt safe in your civilian
arms, and ate my chocolate.
how I wish Ike could be with me now,
now in my finest hour of need-
he'd take me up in those paternal arms
and just hold me just hold me

and tell me how necessary all this was,
and we would cry together
like men who smoked luckies,
and and and i'd show him
my postcards.
I take a GI shit on all of you now,
you gutless Axis cowards,
I hate your fucked-up little hats,
And your full-bird bellies
full of German piss wine-
salute this, you ungrateful picture-takers;
this is my rifle, my great pussy equalizer,
any you cocksuckers want a piece of me now?
I KNOW WHO YOU ARE NOW!
I AM YOURS NOW AND YOU ARE MINE!
(medicine administered 3 Nov 1944)
and I saw a new-fangled heaven,
and a ranch-style earth:
for the German artillery
had reduced the old ones
to rubble and stories
for the grandchildren.

Caterpillar Poem

I feel your calculated issue of unfiltered blood
    as it loses itself in details-
    These are the words you wanted pulled from me,
    so wallow in their thickness,
    splash about in their incremental deaths,
    take pleasure in their liquid martyrdom.
    I will not offer them in this way again.
    This is simple grist for the intellects' greasy mill-
    Those who rape poets for second guesses
    (and come back for sloppy thirds),
    Those who heap nothing but coal and praises
    on the heads of junkies and victims.
    I could have been one of them, I could.
    I could have waxed mysterioso about
    the embarrassed pudenda of beauty
    nothings, who stand and wonder
    how the judges will taste,
    and where mother will hide the crown.
    This is what this art has reduced us to-
    damaged words for a damaged world.
    (There ain't much room for a beat
    when you can't dance to it.)
    What wings I earn will be mine to keep-
    And I have minutes to go before I sleep,
    And I have minutes to go before I sleep...
CUIDADO

all pardons on us, most heavenly father,
for we have had your wives for breakfast.
revolution should be a poor man's fist,
covered in shit and fleeting promises;

we do not deal in subtleties here,
this is not a finishing school.
georgia's beautiful in the summertime,
when young men's fancies turn to rape;
georgia's lovely in the wintertime,
when old despots' thoughts turn to action.
when the peepholes start squealing freedom, freedom-
who am i to stand on their filthy necks,
who am i to display their broken bodies,
who am i to enjoy the fruits of their children?
i am the well-trained way, der Truth, das Light,
no man comes to know power but through me,
i am the grass that grew high at Austerlitz,
(i still work.)
pardons on all of us,
ye heavenly hosts,
for we have used your servants
as bulletin boards...

Surprise Makeover

we tried to stay away
    from anything plum,
    which looks so garish
    in the cold fog
    of authority,
    as the neighbors report
    nothing new between
    those two.
    if you could have seen
    the patches of her
    own hair we found under
    her mother's old wig,
    you'd understand why
    we went with an auburn
    highlight, and avoided
    teasing her too much.
    we left a lot of the blues
    on her face and neck,
    because her fall was inevitable,
    and it's better to anticipate
    a change than
    react too late,
    we reasoned.
    the dress is from the Salvation
    Army, and most women should
    be able to buy it without
    fear of retribution.
    once the cast comes off,
    you'll notice what lovely
    hands she once had,

and how well defensive
wounds take to a neutral
powder base.
just before air,
we noticed
some fresh
puffiness
around the
jawline,
so we tried
toning
her down,
we
tried
toning
her
down.

Snapshot: Kittanning, Pennsylvania, 1963

Looking north up South Water street,
    the dying stand solid as
    parking meters, finding finer spirits
    underground than the ones
    they were promised.
    The stores here are shadowed in,
    windows covered in soap and relocations-
    lonely mothers clutch the gloves
    of those who will soon be from Kittanning.
    A fine layer of dust grows more confident,
    as the Allegheny does its best to carve
    new scars through the Rust Belt's open wounds;
    The sulfur sun finally glazes over a town
    that stays locked away in its own dead storage,
    trapped by the ice cold promise of something
    darker than coal, stronger than steel.

SO WHAT HAVE *YOU* BEEN DOING?

As I take a few reflective sips of coffee this morning, I'm reminded of an impending personal milestone. For reasons which will soon become apparent, I'm tempted to change that to read 'personal MILLstone.'

Next year will mark my twentieth season out of high school. Of course you realize this means plane tickets, ill-fitting suits, complete memory loss, hotel reservations and an open bar. Guess which one will get my fullest attention. It's not that I'm against the need for class reunions on some intellectual plane, but sometimes I question the wholesale marketing of what may be a rather painful yardstick for some. I anticipate receiving quite a few unsolicited invitations from companies who specialize in class reunions. I have a feeling I'm going to separating a little wheat from a boatload of chaff when January arrives.

At first I feared that no one from my class would even find me. I just knew I'd end up on that collective Wanted Poster you always see in the local newspaper. Now with the glories of the Internet in full bloom, my new fear is that EVERYONE will find me. I can't speak for all of you, but don't you sometimes think of your former classmates as perpetual teenagers? My last contact with 90% of my class was in the years of Reaganomics and fluorescent clothing. I'm not sure I'm ready to meet the modern editions who will show up en masse at the one country club in my hometown. I just know I'm going to expect parachute pants and leg warmers a-plenty, while the DJ plays Duran Duran and a Flock of Seagulls.

As badly as I want to meet the accountants, teachers, housewives and small business owners of today, part of me still wants to crawl back into the 80s womb and talk about Luke and Laura's wedding all night. Nostalgia isn't everything, but sometimes it's the thing that will keep you the warmest.

THE GREAT HYMNAL WAR

As I drink my coffee this morning, I think about my pseudo-career in music. I have always been interested in music, ever since I taught myself to play one of those wheezy Magnus chord organs when I was 4. The Magnus people made learning a breeze with their idiosyncratic numbering system. I still enjoy playing 5-6-5-3-5-6-5-3, and that beautiful love ballad 1-4-3-5-3-5. Eventually I took up the clarinet and learned a little something about music theory. Little did I know how much of an impact this early musical education would have on my life.

When I was 12, we joined the pew-jumping, chandelier-swinging church next door to our house. In reality it was an Apostolic Pentecostal church, but you know how rumors get started. The pastor was a firm believer in the encouragement of 'young people', which surely included me at the time. His wife was the church pianist, a young associate pastor was the organist, a family of country singers played guitars and yours truly became- the accordionist. My Magnus chord organ skills payed off in spades as I dutifully plowed through any song mentioning the Blood of the Lamb. One thing about Pentecostal music- the Blood had better be flowing, or else we're not playing it. For the four years I played in that orchestra, I was steeped in foot-stomping, hand-clapping good old gospel music.

Twenty some odd years later I find myself being asked to play the organ for a small country Methodist church in Alabama. Full of my former Pentecostal vim and vigor, I eagerly agreed to take on the challenge. Oh ye of little research. I found myself deeply embroiled in what can only be called the Great Hymnal War. The old hymnals could conceivably be divided into dirge/not dirge, while the absolute newest versions might as well have included 'Jesus is just alright with me'. Somewhere in the middle was the accepted hymnal, which incorporated just enough of both camps to be perfectly contentious to musicians. I'm actually enjoying the schizophrenia, as I quietly plug away on a real church organ every Sunday. But every once in a while,

I find myself wanting to strap on an old accordion and see how strong those ceiling joists really are.

THERE'S MUSIC IN THAT THERE COFFEE, MISTER.

As I settle down to my final cup of coffee for the day, I hear the opening strains of Van Morrison's "Brown-Eyed-Girl" and realize how good life can get. I'm not sure what the most perfect song in the world would sound like, but I think John Prine is going to write it and Van Morrison is going to sing it. If they don't, I'm sure Tom Waits, Bruce Springsteen or Bob Dylan will be on ready five status.

Surprisingly enough, coffee shows up in a lot of memorable songs. Mickey Dolenz promises time for "coffee-flavored kisses and a bit of conversation" in the Monkee's *Last Train to Clarksville*. Don Williams begins his lonesome day with "coffee black, cigarette" in his country hit *Some Broken Hearts Never Mend*. Bob Dylan lingers over *One More Cup of Coffee* before facing (*The Valley Below*).

Oddly enough, I don't believe the Beatles ever mentioned coffee in their music, but one might wonder what was in the cup Paul speaks of in *A Day in the Life*.

Coffee is almost always the one bit of normalcy that creeps into the songwriter's otherwise complicated verses. We can all identify with that desperate search for the waitress, or that early morning jolt of reality only coffee can bring.

For a long time, I thought Van Morrison's *Into the Mystic* was as close to perfection as anyone could get. Now I'm beginning to think that we are all responsible for writing our own perfect song, one where the verses don't really matter and all our friends know the chorus by heart.

YOU KNOW THAT WE ARE LIVING IN A COFFEE WORLD

My wife tells me that she's been drinking coffee since she was four years old, and somehow I believe her. It may be the dozen or so cans of Story House gourmet coffee strewn around the house, or it may be the fact that we are already on our third coffeemaker in six years of marriage. We can't leave the local coffeeshop/bookstore without gazing longingly at the top-end cappucino machines and French press carafes on the shelves. You know those oversized bins of whole bean coffee at the grocery store? I'm beginning to think they're actually free gumball machines for coffee fanatics.

My wife says she started her coffee habit by finishing off the dregs of coffee left behind by her parents. My brother started drinking coffee at our mother's funeral. He started off with equal proportions of cream, sugar and coffee, then eventually acquired a taste for the stronger stuff. Being an inveterate hot tea drinker from way back, I still prefer a little cream and sugar in mine. My first real exposure to coffee was not in a cup, but one of those chewy coffee-flavored candies. I took one bite, expecting chocolate, and received a rather abrupt introduction to the world of coffee.

Some say the world is divided into two groups- those who like Neil Diamond and those who don't. I say that the world can be divided in a different way- the world we knew before coffee, and the one we discovered after that first cup. 'Coffee World' is inherently different- life has a few more edges, a little more color. Like any other first experience, you can sense that an invisible border has been irreversibly crossed, but somehow you don't seem to mind the change. Coffee World can be a challenging place sometimes, but its also worth trying all the way to the dregs.

WHAT'S NEXT—COFFEE-FLAVORED COFFEE?

I've been on a diet for about 6 months now, which explains why I just finished eating a bowl of coffee almond ice cream. Let he who is without carb cravings cast the first Slimfast can. Speaking of diet drinks, I believe more than a few companies have composed coffee-flavored variations on their standard liquid fare. Oh they try to be so clever by calling it 'mocha', but we see through their little ruse.

Over the years, there have been many attempts to blend coffee with another food or beverage. Some have proven hugely successful, while others have fallen a little short of the glory. Coffee ice cream came straight out of the vat with a halo and a large bow saying 'Buy me, I'm terrific!', while the earliest versions of cold cappucinos played cards on the shelves and said 'When you run out of every other drink in the house, you know where I live.' Times have changed, and now frozen or chilled cappucinos are among the most popular drinks in gourmet coffeehouses. Sometimes it just comes down to building the perfect beast and waiting for the right consumers to find it.

As appealing as it sounds, there is one coffee-enhanced beverage I'm glad hasn't made it onto store shelves-Drew Carey's infamous Buzz Beer. For those of you who missed the show, Buzz Beer came about after one of Drew's cronies started drinking coffee between taste tests. The combination proved to be marketable on the show, but I seriously doubt anyone would actually try to duplicate it in real life. Coffee has been used in a lot of strange concoctions, but beer seems to do best on its own. (At least I won't be polishing off a pint of beer pistachio ice cream any time soon). That's okay, though- it leaves more room in the fridge for my card-playing iced cappucino buddies.

THERE'S A DAY FOR THAT

I happen to be the proud owner of the most oxymoronic job title in the world- a professional poet. Historically, this has proven to mean I'll be long gone before the check for the pizza arrives. We poets live for April, which happens to be National Poetry Month. For a solid thirty days, poetry and poets can roam freely in the streets, without calling their parole officers or violating restraining orders.

April also happens to be National Coffee Month, which makes some sort of symbiotic sense to me. Coffeehouses were generally the first venues to embrace poets, so I can see sharing a month with the hands that feed us. All this talk about national months got me to thinking, though. You have to figure that for every month that makes sense (Black History Month, AIDS Awareness Month, Women in Sports Month, etc.) there must be hundreds that are best described as answers to obscure trivia questions. Creating a new 'Month' must be the bread-and-butter of legislators everywhere. It's got to be the best win/win situation of all time- instant respect for the lawmakers, and recognition of the oft-ignored blue-backed iguana owners of America.

I'd like to know who decides what cause deserves a national Day, Week, Month or Year. The negotiations have got to be the most delicate diplomatic operations in Washington DC: 'You know, Bill, I share your love for the little critters myself, but how about National Wombat DAY? We had to give Senator Jones "National Pantyhose Month", so the calendar's looking a little full right now.' No matter what the occasion, I'd like to think someone is waiting for the Wombat Parade of Heroes to pass by on that special day.

All I know is that next April, I will be sipping my gourmet coffee and working on my next collection of poems. If you care to join me, just remember I like extra pepperoni.

COFFEE NIPS: A GATEWAY CANDY?

I realized the other day that my first taste of coffee didn't come from a cup, but from a little piece of penny candy called a Coffee Nip. My dad used to take us to an indoor flea market on Saturdays, and one of the booths featured nothing but candy of every description. If we had a quarter or two, we could easily recreate the average Halloween haul. I fell hard for a piece of German-style chocolate called an Ice Cube. It wasn't like your average Chunky or Hershey Bar- it was incredibly smooth and creamy with a strong hazelnut flavor. At three cents a pop, it was the Cadillac of penny candies but I couldn't get enough of them. Our first and only goal on Saturdays was to seek out the 'Candy Lady' and load up our small brown paper bags.

On other days, we would ride our bikes up to a store called Reinker's, which was owned and operated by a sweet old German man. Mr. Reinker ran his store old-school style, with clerks that always knew your name and the best ice cream section in town. He would always insist on patting us on the head, which would simply offend our four year old sensibilities.

As I grew older, I discovered that Mr. Reinker also stocked an incredible assortment of penny, nickel and dime candies. Just behind the cashier stood the Wall of Paradise, complete with Ice Cubes and Coffee Nips.

But it didn't stop there, no sir. Reinker's carried the Holy Grail of collectibles for an eight year old kid- Wacky Packs. These were cards featuring spoofs of well-known products, like Dunder Bread and A-Jerks Cleanser. Each pack contained the ubiquitous stick of cardboard bubble gum, at least 5 stickers and a piece of a much larger puzzle. It was a glorious day when I actually had enough pieces to finish the mother of all things Wacky- the big puzzle.

I did some checking around the other day and found a supply of Ice Cubes online. They now go for thirty cents a piece. The Wacky Pack manufacturers cranked out their last run sometime in the late 80s or early 90s. The stickers I wasted as a child are now worth a fortune to serious collectors. I could be very sad about these twists of fate, but I'd much rather get another pat on the head from Mr. Reinker as he casually slips another Ice Cube into my mother's purse.